SEARCHING FOR

HER

Jackson Clear

Copyright © 2024 by Jackson Clear.

All rights reserved. No portion of this book may be reproduced in any form without permission from the publisher, except as permitted by U.S. copyright law.

ISBN: 979-8-9856170-0-9

Published by bigQUARK Productions

Author information at www.thisjusten.com

First Edition

For my father, James L,
who allowed me to be who I was
rather than who he might have wanted me to be.

Now that the sky and earth and wind are still,
An beasts and birds are stayed by sleep,
Night leads her starry chariot on its round,
And without waves the sea lies in its bed;
I am awake, I think, I burn, I weep;
and she who is my undoing
Is ever before me to my sweet pain:
War is my state, full of wrath and grief;
And only in thinking of her
do I have some peace.
Thus from the same clear living spring
Flow the sweet and the bitter on which I feed;
One hand alone heals me and stabs me.
And so that my martyrdom may
not reach the shore,
A thousand times a day
I die and a thousand I am born;
So far away am I from my salvation.

                                        Francesco Petrarca

The Prelude

I GUESS YOU COULD SAY IT BEGAN IN APRIL. That is, I believe it is accurate to say it began in April. Oh hell, I don't know. I suppose you could say it started well before then and would arguably (or perhaps *diagnostically* is the more appropriate word) be correct. Does such a journey as the one I am about to relay really "begin" or "end" at one particular point? (A certainty! A certainty! My kingdom for a certainty!) Well, anyway, the first day of April *did* mark the dawn of resolution for change in my life. And my odyssey actually began on that day as well. So that is where *I'm* going to place "the beginning." Of course, having now fixed this point, I can't help but observe that I failed to note the popular significance of this date — and to see it as the ironic, damning omen that I now do — which speaks volumes as to just how distraught and distracted I had become. But such trivialities would not likely have concerned me anyway. By then, I was mad and manic and thinking only of *her*.

In truth, I had functioned relatively well up to and a bit past my graduation from college in '91. Twenty-five years had passed since I'd floated in the blissful ignorance of my mother's womb (forgive me, dear reader, but cliché does hold truth). My cynicism toward contemporary life had reached its nadir. Nearly all relationships of any value (meaning anyone who would put up with me) had fallen by the wayside. The last to go was my friendship with Jack.

As far as looks, Jack could easily have played Shaggy in the movie version of *Scooby-Doo*. His hair was a dingy reddish-brown mop that appeared to have fallen onto his head after being flung from the window of some airborne castle by a scullery maid pinching her nose in revulsion; his dark, scruffy beard was a non-deciduous perennial, which, though I never saw him groom it, was thin, patchy, and always the same length. He was tall and the further up his lanky frame went, the more it stooped in struggle with gravity.

The Shaggy parallel stopped with Jack's eyes, however, which were set wide apart, and the left of which wandered in a creepy, underworldly way. They were also alert like the wily, half-crazed assistant of some Walmart pharmacist. Personality-wise, Jack was not a goosey coward *comme* Shaggy either, but was calm and deliberate. A songwriting, aspiring "alternative rock" band leader, an adequate if somewhat superficial thinker, and a wry observer of the ironic, Jack was the closest thing to an intellectual I knew at the time.

I had known him since my junior year when we were in a secondary discussion group for a Joyce class. He was the only one in the group who seemed to actually think about what he said, so when he made a subtle social overture to me outside class (he shared a sarcastic comment about the Prof.'s hair style, of all things), my response was uncharacteristically positive. We hit it off relatively well in day-to-day pleasantries but were always arguing the opposite point of view intellectually. While I, for example, gloried in the beauty of the language Joyce chose, Jack felt that since Joyce used that very language to attack his oppressors, it undermined whatever beauty there was to it. A real yawner for most folks, admittedly, but we got pretty worked up over such things. Okay, maybe I was the one who got worked up.

Despite this, we managed to remain relatively close until he met Claire. It wasn't the typical "your friend gets a girlfriend and the friendship goes to pot" situation, though. I actually liked Claire. She was a dark and languid beauty with a very small diamond nose stud. I wasn't attracted to her at all because of her spiritually spacy, unkempt, tree-hugging ways, but she could be clever and funny. The problem was Jack and her together. Their mutual affinity for pop culture eventually proved too much for me.

Our final parting came the night we went to see *Slacker*. They had both seen it and, in their eternal drive to bring me into their camp, had persuaded me against my better judgment to go and see it. When I got to their place, Claire wasn't ready, so Jack threw a copy of *Generation X* on my lap. He knew I had been avoiding it because of all the hoopla. Since I had caved-in partially anyway by going to see the movie, the masochist in me said, "Oh, why not make an evening of it?" But when I reached the part where the narrator is picking liposuctioned fat from his dog's nose, I quietly put the book down. After just a moment of sitting there, I realized I was really annoyed. It bothered me so much I wished I had not read it. Agitated though I was, however, I said not a word. I was not up to yet another argument with Jack and was thankful when he asked me nothing.

I said very little on the way to the movie, which neither of them seemed to notice. I was glad they left me alone. I wanted to figure out why what I'd just read bugged me so much. But I could not understand specifically what had upset me, which irritated me even more. We got to the theater and settled in with the rest of our contemporaries, who made up almost the whole of the audience. I had calmed down a bit and had even managed to chuckle like a good sport at a comment Claire made about how my coloring would work well with the tacky brown uniforms the theater employees wore — a cloaked jab about my lack of employment. When the lights went down, the darkness and the glow from the screen relaxed me a little more. Unfortunately, there was the movie to contend with.

As the rambling, aimless story bled onto the screen, my agitation began to grow again. I made it as far as the scene where that reedy, tubercular looking girl tries to sell a pap-smear she claims is Madonna's to her friends. That scene typified all I had grown to loathe about my generation. I asked myself what drove us collectively to this pathetic, apathetic state of mind? Why was the vulgar and irrelevant so fascinating to us? Then, suddenly, I understood just what I hated about it. It was complete self-absorption; extreme egotism cloaked in irony and the perverse preoccupation with the squalid in life. They cynically pointed out these mindlessly inconsequential things supposedly to display the damning relativity of life. But the truth was that they just did it to show how smart they were and to avoid any serious self-examination which might allow them to actually *do* something with their lives.

I sat there no longer seeing the movie, seething over this shameless waste, this giving up before even trying. I fumed in my seat a little longer until I felt an incredible anger at the senselessness of it surge up and overwhelm me. My whole body trembled like rapidly jiggled Jell-O. I was flush and hot and my head throbbed like the tip of a highly-heated Looney Toons thermometer. But though I wanted to scream, to spew the venomous contempt I felt on everyone in the theater, I could not because I was actually so angry that I started coughing and gagging. At this point both Claire and Jack turned to me. When they saw my face, they both went white.

"Are you okay, man?" Jack leaned over and asked in a hurried, anxious whisper.

I choked and hacked a bit more, then — with enormous effort — finally got control of myself and haltingly sputtered:

"Fahuck yeww."

"What?" he started and asked out loud.

"Shhh!" came hissing from all around.

"Fuck you!" I shouted out with wild euphoric relief at my rediscovered ability to speak.

I jumped to my feet, wobbled a bit, then gained my balance and pointed at the screen:

"Fuck this and fuck you, every one of you, if this is all you fucking think of yourselves!"

A pause.

"Shut the fuck up, asshole!" came a snide female voice from the balcony.

"I may be an asshole," I instantly roared back, "but I'm not as big an asshole as anyone who would sit here and watch this shit and think it's in any way funny! You all make me fucking sick!"

"Man, would you just sit down and shut up!" Jack pleaded, tugging urgently at my arm.

"Yeah!" a voice cried out from my left. "Sit down and shut up or get the fuck out, prick!"

"Oh, I'll leave all right! You can have this crap for yourselves! I'm through with this shit… I'm through with you all!"

"Good! Split! Loser!" boomed a deep baritone from the front row.

Everyone laughed. I could not respond. My head was now reeling from the release of so much pent-up passion. I stumbled down the row and up the aisle. An alarmed theater employee met me coming through the door. I shoved him out of my way and went crashing out the front doors and into the night.

Jack did not call for several days. When he finally did, he left a message saying he thought the whole thing was "really fucking lame." I was screening the call, but felt no impulse to pick up and defend myself. I was through with him. Through with everybody. It all made me sick. Everything. I was tired of trying to pretend that I could like it. And I had finally realized that that was what Jack represented for me: my last attempt to fit in.

∼

BEFORE I MOVED TO SEATTLE, everyone warned me about the rain. They were right. It rained for the next six months. It was mind-numbingly constant. But I didn't care. I was provided for financially by a small trust fund set up by my grandparents. They had intended it to help pay for graduate school. When it turned over to me at twenty-five, graduate school was about as likely as a career in Amway. So, I lived modestly and, except for trips to the grocery store, kept to myself.

For a few weeks, I did nothing but sleep 'til noon then sit and watch the rain out my window. In the beginning, I stewed about the theater episode and what had brought me to that point. At first, I was worried about the suddenness and violence of my outburst. But I finally decided it really wasn't so sudden. As I mentioned before, I'd felt a deep-seated distaste for contemporary society and decided I had obviously been suppressing those feelings more than I'd realized. So naturally it would have to have come out at some point. Albeit, it had broken forth... well, a tad *fortissimo*. But then, that was to be expected given the potentially explosive nature of the psyche when repressed.

As to what had actually upset me, I had begun to feel even

more apathetic than those whom I'd condemned. After all, what did anything really matter anyway? Even though I hated what my generation was saying, ultimately, I knew I did not have the strength to fight it. Given the overwhelming tide of mediocrity flooding the world, fighting it was a losing battle, and I felt broken and defenseless against it. So let the whole world slide into a stinking, degenerate swamp of irrelevance. Everything was fucked up, and trying to save it would be futility epitomized.

The weeks grew into months, and to fill the empty hours I tried to read again. I picked up the books I had enjoyed in college and high school and managed to finish a few short stories and even to wade through one or two novels. In the end, though, I hadn't the energy for it. So I started flipping on the TV. Of course, I saw it was still the giddy idiot-savant messenger of the Apocalypse I had already judged it to be; still mindlessly yet distinctly proclaiming the contemporary passion for degrading, eroding, stupefying banality. But, with my attention span so limited and my mind so hungry for anything to chew, even these hopelessly "empty calories" sufficed.

The soap operas were in full swing by the time I was up and eating my Cheerios. At first, I found it difficult to believe there might be people who actually watched them with any kind of sincerity. Some of the story lines were so incredible, so ridiculously fantastic. People from small-town America in love triangles with characters involved in Central American guerrilla warfare. Lovers stranded on desert islands through the scheming of a long lost (though admirably tenacious) family enemy. Pointlessly elaborate, unyielding plots that no one watching could honestly dream of getting caught up in.

Of course, there were the more mundane themes. Some of them never attempted to leave Smalltownsville, USA (save the occasional sally to New York, Los Angeles, or Europe to give the pretentious characters something to lord over their socially oppressed lessers). However, intrigue was provided by the many vicissitudes of love (first love, marriage, affairs, discovery, divorce, re-marriage) under the umbrella of small scale social infighting over everything from race relations to family disintegration. Here, as with the other approach, cliché abounded.

I did not bother criticizing them, though. There was simply too much to attack. It was mental cotton candy. So I just watched them like a child. Surprisingly (at least to me), I soon found myself looking forward to them. I wanted to know what Michael would do when he found out Sarah, his homespun, down-to-earth fiancee, had a sordid, high-flying, bi-sexual past in the pornography industry and was addicted to diet pills? And Sarah's best friend, Camielle: would she confront the step-uncle who had molested her as a child, but now wanted to be godfather to Camielle's love child with the step-uncle's best friend's son, who had recently died from a rare blood disease? These and many more equally elaborate sub-plots enticed me to and through the noon hour.

I began to wake a little earlier so as not to miss the beginning of the one with which I'd started. This resulted in catching the end of the one before and getting interested in it. So I got up even earlier. It wasn't long before my day was filled with watching them. I even started taping ones from other channels and viewing them into the night. I knew it was absurd. I could in no way rationalize what I was doing. I was pursuing something that was the quintessence of all that had driven me away from people. But what did I care? *So I'm into mindless drivel*, I thought. What does it really matter? There was also the fact that I really could not help myself. The one or two times I tried not to watch, I nearly went out of my head. In short, I was addicted.

My addiction did create a problem: though I taped several different shows a day, filling up many hours, I could not tape enough to occupy all my waking moments. I tried watching the ones I'd taped again, but that was unsatisfying. Like chewing gum from the bed post, it lacked the zest and flavor of the initial experience. I yearned, almost lusted for the new episode. This sense of absence was probably the reason I found myself glancing at romance novel covers in the supermarket. I had to pass them on my way to the produce section. Of course, the covers are designed to catch the eye with those strapping chests and heaving bosoms. And, I'm human, so I looked occasionally.

Then late one night, after I had watched my last tape for the day and was in heavy withdrawal, I stopped and picked one up. *I'll just read the summary on the back*, I thought. When a good-looking middle-aged woman passing by gave me a reproachful little smile, I returned it to the rack and scurried off to buy some bananas. Before I left the store, though, I was drawn back again. This time I went around the corner by the magazine stand to make what I fully intended to be only a scan of the contents.

The next thing I knew I was twenty-five pages into the story of a London born, Highlands bound beauty named Penelope whose lavish red hair and independent, audacious spirit were spurned by the locals but admired and desired by the brawny, brooding land-owning citizen called Malcolm. It was trash, and I knew it. But I kept reading. The writing was thin, the characterizations trite. Still, I kept reading. I told myself to put it down. Just put it down and walk away. But I couldn't. I felt ashamed with each page I turned. It was a sin against every aesthetic value I had ever believed in. Had I really become so desperate?

When I crammed two others with equally lurid covers in my bag and left the store without paying, I knew I had my answer.

∼

SEVERAL MONTHS PASSED, and my obsession grew exponentially. I quickly exhausted the supermarket's romance novel supply and graduated to discount book emporiums. Eventually, I just made several indiscriminate large purchases and had them delivered to me. Throughout my apartment were stacks of read and to-be-read books, from which I selected and read voraciously whenever I had a spare moment.

Of course, recording and following twelve different daily soaps meant spare moments were rare. I had to buy another VCR and TV to accomplish this stressful task. The planning involved for recording was difficult enough, but the execution of the plan was even worse. Since I couldn't stand having to run through the end-of-the-hour commercials with each and every show, I decided to stop and restart the tape on the hour. But I often got so wrapped up in the show I was watching, I sometimes forgot to restart them. Missing the beginning was absolutely maddening because cliffhangers from the day before were often picked up at the start. If you missed them, you had to spend the rest of the time listening for characters to talk about what had happened. Obviously, this sapped much of the fun out of watching.

So I became fanatical about this hourly stop/restart. I vigilantly monitored the clock while still trying to concentrate on whichever show I was watching. This meant the tension mounted as the top of the hour approached and my attention grew disconcertingly divided. By the time the last episode came on, the hourly rise and fall of my heartbeat had nearly worn me out. Then there were the stories themselves that kept me vacillating between high states of anxiety, anticipation, and exhilaration, as well.

Given the above stress, in addition to my irregular eating and sleeping habits, I began to deteriorate physically. I knew it was happening, but nothing mattered to me except doing what I was doing. Occasionally, I had glimpses of how insane it all would seem to an outside observer. But even those moments of clarity did not dissuade me. In fact, the whole thing began to assume the quality of a mission. I started to sense some as-yet-unexplained reason for my obsession, a purpose which would transcend whatever superficial appearance of lunacy there was to it. This belief compelled me toward whatever end — and subsequent explanation — awaited me. And it was not long before I got my answer.

∽

I HAD STAYED UP READING INTO THE NIGHT. At around three in the morning, the lights went out. I had reached a highly dramatic section of the story, so I nearly flew into a rage at this preposterous interruption. I leaped up and began frantically searching for a flashlight. I quickly found one under the kitchen sink, only to discover that the battery was dead. And, of course, I had no replacements. I threw it against the wall, shattering it into pieces and ran outside in some crazed hope of finding light to read by. It had been raining all day and was coming down heavily when I went out. But this did not stop me. I ran around half the night, hoping to find some section of town where lights were on, but I never did.

By the time I got back to my place, I was soaked and shivering and already had a fever. The lights were on by then, but I didn't care. I fell onto my bed and into a week's worth of fever-driven hallucinations. Soft-spoken voices telling disjointed stories of lovers swirled through my torrid mind. Eventually, all other forms and voices left save one: the obscured face of a young woman hovering just above my bed, mouthing something to me that I could not make out. She seemed to be beckoning me, calling for help. When I reached for her, she fluttered and dissipated like an image from a disturbed pool of water. But she would soon return, drifting slowly back together just as she had gone away, then would continue calling me.

As the fever broke and I regained full consciousness, I did not forget the image of this strange, ghostly woman. In fact, I found I could think of nothing else. I wondered incessantly about what it might mean that she appeared to me in apparent distress. I was so distracted I could not get back into my soaps or novels. The more I thought about her, the more real she started to become until, finally, I actually *did* think of her as being alive in the present moment.

Even as I first thought this, I knew it was wildly insane. But then, I thought immediately, why did it have to be insane? Why couldn't this be what my whole obsession had been about? Maybe destiny *had* reached through that ridiculous medium of popularized romance to speak to me of something more profound; of a lover not only waiting for me, but in need of me right now. Not some shallow or common love like I had been watching and reading of, but that harmony of spirits displayed in the greatest of art, existing only in souls capable of deep understanding. A transcendent love, a love capable of buoying me up in life's sea-changes, as well as one that could serve as a foundation for the superstructure of my complicated nature. Never mind if this had all been a part of the clichés I had been feeding on. I now saw the kernel of truth which lay hidden in the husk that was the foundation upon which the contemporary artifice of love had been built.

But what was the distress that dearest of souls, *my* Love, was in? In what way would it manifest itself? I started thinking of the world with which I now had almost no interaction. I recalled a sad and sick place, devoid of hope. This concerned me deeply. What could a beautiful, smart, and — most importantly — savvy young woman (for that was how I was sure she was) do in such a time? It was doubtful she would pursue the particular, admittedly warped, path that I had chosen. I did not doubt, however, that she would be led to an extreme of her own sort, given that we would be so alike. So, what did that leave for her?

As I lay down to try to sleep that night, this was the question that plagued me. And no sooner had I closed my eyes than I began to picture large hairy arms and cumbersome hands passing slowly over the love-of-my-life's nakedness. My eyes popped open. Yet still, in the darkness, I began to see her evenings started in chic nightclubs and ended in her conquest's arms, watching the sunrise over an indifferent cityscape. I was tortured by seductive glances caught in an art gallery and fulfilled in a handy janitor's closet. Drinking, drugs, and strange conversations (the contents of which she would probably never share with me) were the ornaments I saw decorating her life. And these were but a sampling of the parade of corruption that stomped down the Main Street of my mind.

I jumped up and ran from my apartment in hopes of leaving these images behind. Though I roamed around town all day and night to try and forget, my head still boiled with these painful mental concoctions. I knew that she chose this life only to keep off the pain she felt from a lack of me. But this was still too bitter a pill to swallow, which kept me running away.

Finally, as I staggered along near the water in the dark hours of early morning, the jumbled voices in my head gained a single piercing voice and screeched in my mind like an unwatched tea kettle:

"DO SOMETHING!"

"But what... what can I possibly do?" a small, helpless voice answered back. This question echoed through my head and forced the screeching to recede out through my ears into the darkness.

Silent hours passed. I sat in gray pre-dawn light looking out at the calm, dark Sound, sallow and exhausted from lack of food and sleep. The piercing voice had begun again, but now came from a distance like a lonesome factory whistle. It would soon be upon me, repeating itself with the same unrelenting force. I felt desperate to escape, but I knew that to run would be futile. So I simply sat and waited.

That was when it happened. My eyes closed as the sun rose on that virginal April morning, and a small but resolute voice whispered from in front of me:

"Find her."

I did not jump. I did not move at all except to open my eyes. I stared straight ahead, fixed on a point on the edge of the horizon from which I waited for this new voice to emerge. And just as my eyes began to lose focus from staring so long at the same point, the voice came again, only this time stronger and not from in front but behind:

"Find her!"

I leaped to my feet and spun around. No one was there. But it did not matter. I now understood the words. I had been wrong to revert to mere existence, giving up on hope for life with meaning. The voice was telling me, commanding me to follow my destiny. Purpose existed; I just had to pursue it. My goal, my only salvation, was to go out and find my Love and stop her before she ruined herself for me.

∼

WHEN I GOT HOME THAT MORNING, I stormed around my apartment in hot footed preparation to leave (though to just where I knew not) for a good hour before I finally noticed the message on my answering machine. This was such a rare occurance in those recent months that I decided to give it a listen. The message (from my father — profound disappointment: my Darling, why couldn't it, somehow, some inexplicable yet harmonious way, have been you!) went as follows:

"Spencer, I just got in from Washington and, um... I need to see you as soon as possible. Don't bother calling me back tonight... I've got a... benefit dinner to go to that I... I just can't get out of, son. Just pack a bag and catch the next flight down here as quickly as you can. I'll explain everything once you get here."

His faltering voice and almost apologetic tone (a tone I had never before heard from him) shook me from one distracted state of mind into another. I sat on the floor by the answering machine repeating the message over and over while wondering what could have rattled my father, the imperturbable prototype Ken doll, that could have anything to do with me. Though my recent revelation was stamping its feet like a spoilt child demanding to be addressed, my father's obvious distress piqued my curiosity too much to ignore. I had to go and find out what was up.

As I packed, then cabbed it to the airport, I thought about my father's life, which seemed to form a circle in my mind. From what he had told me, his childhood had been idyllic. A tree house, a faithful Springer spaniel named Alfred, fresh-baked pies to steal from the window every Monday afternoon, and Little League baseball every other day in summer. These things and more supposedly made up my father's early Norman Rockwell-like life.

My grandparents — whom I recall as two flatulent but otherwise taciturn, white-haired, wrinkled people who lived in a large, musty-smelling house I visited for one boring hour a month in my childhood — were strict but loving. They raised my father in an upper-middle-class home with a strong sense of right and wrong. This gave him something concrete to rebel against in his impassioned youth, as well as something solid to quietly return to in adulthood.

In '57, his sophomore year in college, a copy of *On the Road* fell into his hands and fanned the nascent disillusion rising in his twenty-year-old breast. During the next summer vacation, he bummed across the country, living from odd job to odd job (adding the money he earned to that which he received from his parents), pursuing whispers of the growing Beat movement. He ended up in San Francisco, where he hung out in bars and coffeehouses listening with fiery eyes to secondhand accounts of readings by Ginsberg, Kerouac, and the like. This summer experience fueled the fires of his rebellion, and when it came to an end, he begrudgingly went back to school at his parents' behest. But when he graduated two years later (ranked around the middle of his class), he decided to tear off against his parents' wishes into the great wide world and see what he could see while living the reckless, carefree life extolled by the Beats.

Seven months later, he sat emaciated and dead broke in a rat-infested hotel in Mexico City. His parents refused to send any more money unless he promised to return and go to law school. Having heard talk of civil rights abuse during his travels through the South, he was able to rationalize his sellout by convincing himself that this higher cause awaited him. He came back and enrolled at Georgetown to study civil law. There he was bitten by the political action bug. He graduated in '62 and plunged immediately into the emerging Civil Rights Movement. A year or so later, he returned to California and took part in the Free Speech Movement at Berkeley. According to him, these were my father's halcyon days, brimming with Homeric drama and excitement. He felt that everything from the tragedies of JFK's assassination and the Vietnam War to the eventual triumph of Civil Rights legislation was interconnected, giving the era an awe-inspiring (pardon me while I yawn) epic quality.

During these glory days, he met my mother. She was beautiful and intelligent, and, most importantly to him, she had a sympathetic ear. They met at a rally at which he had given an impromptu speech. Afterward, he said, she sought him out to compliment him. They went out for drinks, slept together later that night, and were married two months later. Five years after that, when I was four, she left him.

Her abrupt departure must have left him reeling; he remained single for twelve years. He did finally remarry a woman fifteen years his junior named Natalie. She was a beautiful, articulate idealist fresh out of the JFK school of politics at Harvard, who worked on his research staff. From what I know, he has remained essentially true to her, and she has continued to be a key player in his team approach to life. That life now consists of lobbying "for the environment" in state and federal capitals, then coming home (in California) to Natalie and five-year-old Jeffery (my step-brother) on various weekdays and occasionally for a whole weekend: by all appearances, an ideal existence.

~

I CAUGHT A FLIGHT EARLY THAT MORNING, which arrived in Sacramento around nine, and went directly to my father's office. When I walked into the reception room, Jane, his secretary, was on the phone laughing. She was a full-figured redhead in her late thirties, still stunningly attractive, albeit conventionally so. I had always tried to flirt with her in spite of the fact that she all but ignored me. Before I could start anything, however, she stopped speaking as soon as our eyes met and intently watched as I walked by. Her expression puzzled me; it seemed a look of pity. I was so used to no response from her that this reaction threw me for a second. But I recovered quickly with an impish grin and a quick wink, then fluttered my fingers to wave as I walked past to my father's office.

The office was suffused with sunlight which streamed in through large plate glass windows, tumbled onto the deep blue carpet, cascaded up and through the non-glare glass of framed paintings by Chagal and sketches by Picasso, then finished with a splash off the leaves of various plants placed discriminately about the room. The walls were filled with his numerous awards and commendations (for what, I could not say), as well as pictures of him with various dignitaries, minor heads of state, and sundry celebrities.

My father sat behind a large, modern, oak desk, talking adamantly but with apparent good nature on the phone. On the desk-high file cabinets behind him was a vase brimming with flowers arranged in disheveled perfection and a picture of Natalie and Jeffery in the Alps, bundled up in ski clothes and waving to the camera with wild enthusiasm. He had paused momentarily to listen, so when he saw me, he hesitated slightly, then smiled a warm, broad smile, motioning me with almost melodramatic exuberance to one of the two enormous white leather chairs before his desk. As I sat down, I noticed again his square jaw and his bright, penetrating blue eyes. But his skin, which was once taut, was growing slack and wrinkled, and, though the good looks of his youth could still be easily discerned, they had waned and now served more as an expression of his mortality.

After twenty minutes of watching him gesture this way and that as he lightheartedly but relentlessly cajoled a potential contributor, he hung up the phone. His smile lugubriously drooped as he regarded me for an awkward moment of silence in which my irritation at being put off so long achieved full bloom.

"How are you, son?" he asked, cautiously.

"Hey, what the hell's going on?" I barked. "I don't hear from you for forever, then you call me up and get me down here with no explanation as to why I'm supposed to come, and now I'm getting some kind of pathos-laden greeting from both you and your secretary."

"I'm sorry, son," he said in a hang-dog way. "It's just that this type of situation is one I'm not very good at, and I don't know quite how to deal with it."

He looked so downcast I felt bad for having snapped at him.

"Well, what is it, Dad?"

I threw the "Dad" in to try and make up for my curtness. For a moment, his eyes brightened a bit, but then he looked out the plate-glass windows, and his face took on a dreamy, melancholy expression.

"Son," he said, which annoyed me, since he deployed the

term only in prelude to some unsolicited piece of advice. "I've got some bad news, and I'm struggling to find a way to tell you without upsetting you any more than necessary."

He looked at me with that pathetic expression for a few moments and then, sensing my rising irritation, blurted out:

"Your mother is dead."

He seemed to study my face for a reaction, but when he saw none, he continued hesitantly.

"I received the news just yesterday. I don't know why, but she made me the executor of her will."

Here he stopped again and looked at me closely.

"Are you all right?" he asked.

"I'm fine," I said evenly. "Tell me what you know."

He seemed to grow uncomfortable, squirming in his chair before he leaned over, thumbed through a stack of papers on the desk, pulled out two documents, and set one of them in front of me. He waited a moment, I assume, to allow me to pick up these papers. But after I made no move, he looked at me as though a little confused, then readjusted his position in preparation to speak.

"These were faxed to me yesterday," he began in a subdued tone. "She was living in France, just outside of Paris. This is a letter from a French law firm." He shook the paper in his hand slightly without looking up. "It seems the circumstances around her death are still not very clear, but they suspect..." he paused here and cleared his throat, "...they suspect that she was drinking and lost control of her car."

Here he stopped again and eyed me over the edge of the papers. I sat silently, waiting for him to continue.

"I'm sorry, son," he said softly, looking at me with a pity I instantly detested. When he saw I was not going to respond, a wounded expression passed fleetingly over his face.

"Be all that as it may," he said, "there's another issue I have to tell you about. One that I hope will bring some light into this gloomy circumstance of yours."

"I don't know quite how," he said, in a tone marked by a lightness that stuck me as perverse compared to the sullen one he had just been using, "but it appears your mother came into quite a lot of money in the years since… well, since we last heard from her."

"Since *you* last heard from her," I falsely corrected him, since I hadn't seen or heard from her either.

"Yes, well, whatever," he said with obvious impatience. "The bottom line is that your mother has left you some money, Spencer. In fact, it's quite a lot of money…"

At this point my father's voice suddenly sounded as though all the bass and most of the volume had been sucked out of it. When he opened his mouth, all I could hear was what sounded like the high-pitched buzzing of a small fly. He sat in front of me making gestures, looking from me to the papers, then back to me with that fly voice. I began to look at him intently, squinting in an effort to try to understand what he was saying. He buzzed on for what seemed an hour. My head began to ache from the intense concentration. Though he appeared to notice, as I guessed from the occasional flickers of irritation and uncertainty on his face, he was evidently trying to ignore my expression. Suddenly his voice ballooned up and boomed as he said:

"...it all appears legitimate and, though some of it is in real estate and thus not liquid, it totals, roughly, two-point-one million dollars."

At this sentence, I smiled, coughed, then tumbled forward out of my chair. I'd been leaning further and further forward in a strain to decipher what he was saying so, realizing it was just a silly little accident, I decided to lay there a moment to get my bearings. My mother's executor did not take it so lightly. He jumped up from his chair, and I saw an expression of shock, almost terror, etched on his face as he peered over his desk at me. I smiled weakly and waved to try to comfort him.

"Jesus, Spencer!" he shouted. "Jane! Jane, bring some water in here! Spencer's fainted!" He then bounded over to help me up.

"I was worried you might take it like this!" he cried.

He looked agitated, but I sensed a certain satisfaction in him at being able to come to my aid.

"I'm fine," I said with an air of indifference, brushing away his groping, helpless hands as I sat up and dragged myself back into the chair. I admit I felt a little shaky, but I didn't like the idea of him helping me.

He was hovering over me like a fretful mother hen when Jane rushed in with the ordered a glass of water. I drank slowly, looking at them serenely over the edge of the glass as they stood anxiously watching. I began to regain my composure.

They continued to exchange nervous but significant glances. My mind grew clearer in the following minute or so of silence. Just as my father seemed about to speak, I raised my hand to stop him and asked in a calm, clear voice:

"How much cash is it, exactly?"

He hesitated, then traded another anxious glance with Jane.

"The figure I gave you was before taxes," he said with a tremor of insecurity in both his voice and eye, "but after taxes there will be... approximately... one-million-one-hundred-forty-seven-thousand dollars in cash and three-hundred-and-fifty-two-thousand in blue chip stocks and bonds with the remaining value lying in the real and personal assets."

"Where is the cash?" I asked, again after a pause.

"It's in a numbered Swiss bank account," he answered in the same wavering tone.

"Do you have all the information concerning this here?"

"Yes, everything has been sent to me."

"And you have copies for me?"

"Yes, I have a folder for you with everything in it. Spencer, you don't look good... what are you thinking?"

He said this breathlessly, as though frightened by how I might respond. I ignored his question and asked in a light, assured tone with a simple smile:

"Could I have that folder, please?"

He made a slight gesture of protest but then noted my expression and understood I would discuss nothing. Turning dejectedly, he walked round his desk, bent down, and pulled a manila folder from a drawer. I stood up and reached across the desk for it.

A strange thrill of exhilaration coursed through me as I gripped the folder tightly. A dam had broken in my brain, and a cold lucidity was flooding its every cell. I could see what was happening with absolute clarity. In this admittedly peculiar and oblique way, my mother was giving me the means to pursue my true Love. As the only thing that mattered to me was finding my Love, the money itself was irrelevant. I saw it rather as an instrument — a weapon even — I would use in my quest to cut through any obstacles placed before me. And what a weapon! Given the God-like nature of money in America (and the majority of the world, for that matter), I could command respect and use this power to pursue my Love wherever fate deemed necessary.

I saw the moment for definitive action had come. I jumped to my feet and dashed past Jane and my father, nearly knocking them down in the process. I could not be bothered with inconsequential pleasantries. I burst out of the office and careened down the stairs to the street, my father's voice echoing my name after me.

∼

WHEN I REACHED MY HOTEL, I told the desk clerk I was not to be disturbed for any reason, giving him a hundred dollars to ensure this, and went to my room to chart my course of action. It did not take long to comprehend the immense difficulty of my task.

I did not know my Darling's name, what city she lived in, or even what country for that matter. I had a general idea of what she would look like, but was vague on her exact height, weight, eye, and hair color. Of course, I did not let these little encumbrances stop me. Obviously, certain things could quite easily be ruled out. This was the case with the exact city and country she lived in. Naturally, the number to omit was much larger than that to be considered, a major relief to my overtaxed brain. And it wasn't long before I realized that, although this woman would be dreadfully international in her orientation and extremely well-traveled, *ma petite femme* was undoubtedly American; for she would have to understand, in the way only an American woman would be able, the strange complexities of me, her American man.

With that in mind, I took out a map of these United States and began to cross off various areas of the country based on their stereotypes alone. I contended that if certain beliefs about a place had been held long enough to become stereotypes, there must be a large amount of truth to them. Through this process of elimination, I was surprised to see how quickly I ferreted out the only state in which my dearest would live: California. I decided that despite all the derisive comments made about it by various Easterners and comics, millions of Asians and Hispanics could not be wrong, and I knew my future bride would be wise enough to see this. I was also pleased by the coincidental fact that I was in the capital of that very state.

It then became necessary to prioritize certain sections of the state. The Central Valley and the extreme north were places I immediately placed at the bottom of the list. Although she might have originated from these regions, the acute difference between herself and those with whom she would have been required to live would have forced her to migrate to someplace where at least a few people around her noticed the sardonic behavior she exhibited towards them and society in general (my poor jaded girl). She would invariably avoid the mountains and deserts because, although certainly self-sufficient, she would be far from the rugged type. With all this in mind, I decided to start in San Francisco, the proximity of which made the beginning of my journey only an hour or so drive away. From there I could proceed down the coast, possibly taking time to explore some interior regions if I reached Los Angeles. Then all the way to the Mexican border, if necessary.

These logistical aspects settled, I began to consider the equipment necessary to snare my Darling. She could, of course, be moving in just about any social circle, and so, given the cornucopia of images from which to choose among the American people-scape, I was at first baffled as to what type of persona I should assume to attract her most. But knowing you catch more flies with honey than with vinegar, I decided that, at least initially, I would flaunt my recently acquired riches in hopes that, like the peacock, an ornate plumage would help gain my prize.

After calling Switzerland and having the bank wire all the cash to my personal account, I phoned the credit card companies. From American Express, I demanded a Platinum card;

from the Gold divisions of Visa and Mastercard, I flatly stated my expectation of a twenty-five-thousand-dollar credit limit per card. I gave my bank account number to each bewildered customer service representative, telling all three that I expected their respective cards to be waiting at the Fairmont concierge desk when I reached San Francisco the next evening. I then called the local Mercedes dealership and asked if they had a black 500 SL in stock. A smug, unctuous salesman told me one just happened to be available at that moment and wryly asked if I would like to reserve it. I coolly told him yes, gave him my name and account information, and told him to draw up the papers and have the car waxed, gassed, and ready to go in an hour.

As I hung up the phone, emotions passed through me like slow waves of heat. I felt an odd sort of certainty in my uncertainty. I knew I was doing the right thing, that finding my Love was my only hope in life. But I felt unsure as I stood before a dark, unknown future. Knowing my capricious Darling was my only guiding light was no solace either. Could I find her? How would I know her? If I found her, would she recognize in me all that I saw and so desperately needed in her?

When I snapped from my reverie, the prescribed hour had elapsed. As I intended to buy a new persona in the City, I left everything but the folder my father had given me, some basic toiletries, and the clothes on my back in the hotel room. I went to the dealership where I met the formerly chilly salesman, whose light step and all-too-ready gracious smile betrayed a thinly cloaked exuberance. While signing the financial and insurance papers, I treated him to the same smugness with which he had initially greeted me. I drove off the lot in a triumphant, euphoric haze and headed to the road to find my one hope, my only happiness, my one and only true Love.

PART I
THE SEARCH BEGINS

I WAS ON THE ROAD AROUND 2:00, but encountered trouble from the onset. Only a half an hour after I'd began my quest, my newly purchased wonder of Bavarian engineering died on me. Being mechanically obtuse, I made no attempt to find the problem, let alone fix it. Instead, I negotiated the racing traffic to the other side of the road and headed back to the last off-ramp I had passed. Although cars were screaming by at seventy-plus miles per hour, I still held out my thumb in hopes that the pathetic sight of me trudging along in the middle of nowhere might germinate some latent seed of philanthropy in one of those destination-obsessed drivers and compel them to stop and give me a ride.

After only a few minutes, a tan, mid-eighties Plymouth J car pulled over. I ran up to the passenger side, my faith in at least the potential for human goodness somewhat restored. The driver was in his late forties to early fifties, balding, and had on large, thick, rimless glasses. He was a big man, probably two-hundred-fifty pounds and easily over six feet tall. He wore a white, short-sleeved, button-down collar shirt, a pair of black polyester pants, and an unearthly look of placid self-assurance.

"Thanks for stopping," I said, panting breathlessly as I got in.

"It's my pleasure," he responded in a round, measured tone.

"In fact," he added, "it's my duty to help a person in need."

He had his arm on the back of the seat with his body turned slightly towards me and was looking at me almost like a father who's found his child doing something both he and the child knew shouldn't be done. I say he was looking at me, but, because of the thickness of his glasses, he actually appeared to be gazing off over my shoulder. I thought the last comment odd and felt awkward as he continued to stare at me in silence. But I then remembered my Darling was waiting and became resolute:

"I'm sorry, but I'm kind of in a hurry," I said. "You can drop me off at the next exit. I'll be fine from there."

"Yes, I'm sure you will be," he said calmly as he turned away and put the car in gear.

As we merged into traffic, I was wondering if I had gotten myself mixed up with some sort of altruistic nut-case when he turned to me, smiled serenely, and said:

"You have nothing to fear. I'm not going to harm you."

If I was feeling nervous before, this statement did nothing to help things. I quickly assessed him out of the corner of my eye. He did not seem particularly menacing. Kind of big and goofy looking, actually. Still, something was unsettling about him. Even from the side, the look of certainty that had been in his eyes when I got in was still there. This troubled me. I had seen that look somewhere before, maybe in documentaries about Mao or Khomeni. Then the last comment. It intensified the weird feeling he gave me. But even though I had grown very uncomfortable in this short space of time, I did not let on. He was in control of when, where, and how we were to stop. So I decided to use the naturalist approach, treating him as I would some animal I had happened upon in the wild, with feigned indifference and nonchalance.

"It's not you I'm worried about," I finally responded after a moment, struggling in spite of myself to sound casual. "It's just that I've got something important I've got to take care of, so I'm a little on edge right now."

He said nothing, looking over instead with that disturbingly benign smile. I fidgeted and actually felt cold sweat beading up on my forehead. I tried to calm myself. It was ridiculous to get so upset over this guy. He did not look the part of a homicidal maniac. Of course, I immediately wondered, what would a homicidal maniac look like? In fact, maybe he looked exactly the part. The innocent-faced insurance salesman type might be the perfect ploy to lull potential victims into his car. Before I could get myself truly worked up over this prospect, however, he spoke and derailed this line of thought.

"Son," he began in an authoritative tone, "just what, may I ask, is your present relationship with the Lord?"

I looked over at him to see if he was serious. His smile remained the same as before, but his eyes had narrowed purposefully, as though he saw some goal in the distance he was convinced he could obtain. So strange and frightening was his expression that I wondered for a moment if I could survive a leap from the car. But as we were just then moving with the seventy-mile-an-hour flow of traffic, I had to dismiss that option.

"Ah, I, ah, can't say as I have one," I stammered.

"*That*," he said with grave emphasis, "is a woeful reply."

We then began to accelerate slowly but markedly. I saw my off-ramp coming up, so I decided to define the situation and find out if I was as much a captive as I had begun to feel.

"Ah, excuse me, but I'll need you to let me off…"

"Son," he interrupted, "do you ever think about eternity?"

With this question, I finally saw the light. I was in the car with a fired-up evangelist who, judging by these preliminary inquiries, was hell-bent on saving my soul. Although this created a sense of panic in me, I also experienced a sort of calm in understanding the situation. The calm took a back seat to the panic, however, when we began to swerve in and out of lanes, forcing me to grip the passenger door armrest with all my might to keep from sliding off the seat.

"We often don't think about eternity, or where we'll be in it until it's too late," he now thundered, "but the Lord Jesus Christ has thought it out for you already, son."

This statement marked the commencement of a well-rehearsed string of rhetorical questions of hope and salvation: Did I know that He had died for me? Was I aware that I had only to ask Him into my heart? He did not look at me as he spoke but rather stared straight ahead, transfixed by the goal he had set and was now trying to reach. Though I continued to try to appear calm, my mind ran frantically, hunting for any viable means of escape. While doing so, I glanced for the first time at the floorboard behind the front seat. I saw several large rectangular pieces of posterboard mounted on sticks. We suddenly hit a bump and one of these signs fell over, confronting me with the picture of a bloody aborted fetus and the words, "This Is A Choice."

"Jesus Christ!" I screamed without thinking.

The Evangelist appeared as though he'd been struck by an unabridged Bible cast down from on high; he turned abruptly to me with a look of shock and confusion on his face. I don't know how, but in that split second, I saw my chance for escape.

"Oh, help me now, Jesus Christ!" I cried out again, this time as if I believed the words I was saying with all my heart.

He appeared unsure of what to make of me, looking nervously from me back to the road then to me again. Without taking my eyes off him, I made my face a mask of plaintive desperation. This was the decisive blow. His lower lip began to quiver as he regarded me with triumph and pity. The car began to decelerate.

"*He* is there for you, son; you need only ask," cried the Evangelist, his voice quaking with emotion.

"I want to kneel down. I want to kneel down and ask!" I shouted, while maintaining the expression that had brought my victory.

We quickly crossed four lanes of traffic and took the next exit. The J car slid to a stop in a dirt turnout. I quickly rolled down my window, opened the door, then hopped out, slamming the door behind me.

"I need a Bible!" I pleaded as I stuck my head back inside the car, "Please, give me a Bible!" I knew I didn't really need to do this, but I now felt safe and had actually gotten into the whole charade.

"I knew I could reach you!" he hollered as he dug down under his seat and pulled out a pocket-sized New Testament, which he laid in my out-stretched hand. "I could see by the look in your eye that you were on a spiritual pilgrimage."

In the next few moments, at last, I could refrain from smiling no longer.

"It was a spiritual goal you were trying to reach, wasn't it?" he asked with sudden uncertainty and suspicion.

"Oh, sure, I was in need. Thanks for saving me!" I shouted as I continued to smile. Now safe outside the J-car, I was unafraid of him noticing my sardonic tone. He frowned as I waved, turned and started jogging to a phone booth I saw at a gas station in the distance.

The Evangelist, frothing at the mouth in a righteous fury, pulled-up beside me.

"You'll burn in Hell for mocking the Lord," he boomed out while shaking his fist at me.

I jogged on, ignoring him.

"The Lord, our God, will not be ridiculed by a smart mouth like you!" he blared in a towering wrath.

"Whatever," I shrugged and continued on.

"We'll just see about that!" he roared. With that, he jerked the car into a turn and sped off toward the freeway entrance.

I was only a hundred yards or so from the gas station and was feeling a bit winded, so I decided to walk the rest of the way. I had gone only a few steps, however, when I heard the whine of a six-cylinder engine behind me. I turned to see the Evangelist's car bearing down on me full bore. In an instant, I leaped out of the way, rolling down an embankment and into a chain-link fence at the edge of a shopping center parking lot next to the road. I heard the car tires spin out in the dirt, then heard several cars screech to a stop on the pavement. Scrambling up the embankment, I saw the Evangelist sitting in his car across the road, wearing a malevolent, victorious smile.

"It seems," he gloated, his eyes gleaming with vindictive scorn, "that we are not quite so confident in ourselves in the face of Divine retribution."

"But the Lord has seen fit to give you your youth and agility," he cooed. "He has allowed you to escape your just rewards. Do not, my son, waste this Divine reprieve. Read the Lord's word, which I now see you gripping so fervently, and with an open heart and true sincerity come into the fold."

By this point, cars were gathering behind him, honking as drivers howled malicious threats at him. I stood clutching that New Testament as he waved and pulled slowly away with reborn serenity on his face.

The Mercedes people were extremely apologetic. While admitting no fault, they quickly dispatched a flatbed truck to pick both me and the car up. When I arrived at the dealership, they saw me and assumed my frazzled appearance and highly agitated manner were due to their product's failure. After watching me feverishly pace the waiting room floor for almost an hour, the service department manager took pity on me and asked if there was any way he could help relieve my obvious distress. But before I could answer, a youthful-looking, middle-aged mechanic in a spotless gray jumpsuit ambled in and dryly reported:

"It vas only a broken van belt."

My mood was sour when I left the dealership, and it absolutely plunged when I mistakenly took a freeway heading east, which I realized only after it was too late, was different from the one the Mercedes people advised me to take. I cursed and railed for several minutes and was just about to pull over to take a closer look at the map when I saw a sign for San Francisco. My error, as it turned out, would lead me over the Golden Gate Bridge. Before my little episode with the Evangelist, I had considered taking this route, since so many successful adventures had begun there. But when the Mercedes people lined me out in the other direction, I forgot about my plan. Now, however, I saw fate had intervened and had most certainly played a role in my mistake. I took it as auspicious, and my spirits rose substantially.

And when that magnificent structure spanning the Gate finally stretched forth below me, I experienced something akin to euphoria. I rolled across the bridge and could not keep my eyes off The City, which glistened in the sunlight like a bejeweled crown. San Francisco: another name for *it*; so California sophisticated; so West Coast cosmopolitan; undoubtedly one of the hippest cities in the land. Full of shit though they might have been, the beatniks at least knew this. A city of immigrants, a city of artists, a world port with skyscrapers like pyramids and streets great and small, all brimming with character and characters. The most bars per block of any city in the world is one rumor I'd heard about San Francisco. True or not, if there was any city my Darling was likely to be in, this was it.

I checked into a suite at the Fairmont by late afternoon, bought some ridiculously priced sweats from the hotel gift shop, then dined in my room. Though I was excited to be on the trail of my Love at last, I decided to lay low and regain my spirits completely in order to begin my quest the next day in a thoroughly clear frame of mind. Patience, I felt, would be a key element to success. I took a long, hot bath after dinner, during which I thought with relief of the life I was leaving behind. All its emptiness and drudgery were in the past. But, in spite of this relief, another heaviness visited me again. I could not stop thinking of her and where she might be. While it gave me a thrill to think she could be so near, I had to fight the fear that I might not find her, that she might somehow elude me. Later, with these thoughts in mind, I wriggled down into my luxurious bedding and slipped off into fitful dreams.

I awoke around nine the next morning. After a quick breakfast, took a limo to Nordstrom, I. Magnin, Saks Fifth Avenue, and various specialty shops where I outfitted myself in Cannali, Armani, and the like. The salespeople fell all over themselves helping me and were only too happy to meet my demands. I had one particularly chic Armani suit prepared for me while I waited, and had the rest of my purchases sent to my suite, saying I wanted it all there by the next afternoon. A few tactfully distributed hundred dollar bills helped accomplish this with alacrity. It was near evening when I sent the limo away, having decided to get a feel for the City on my own. Thus prepared, I hit the streets to begin searching for her.

I decided my perfidious Dear would no doubt have been inhabiting the environs of some bar since early afternoon, so I knew I'd have to find where the hippest happy hour happened to be. I walked up to Union Square and flagged a cab, hoping to get a driver who knew the place to go.

"Where to?" asked a narrow-faced unshaven cabby as I jumped in.

"Wherever the coolest happy hour in the City is."

Without missing a beat, he jerked the car into gear and bolted out into the racing traffic. From Union Square, we sped upward and west. With surgical skill, he cut through small gaps between cars and dodged pedestrians, whom he cursed in a low but audible voice for venturing into his path. If a car in front of us stopped for anything but a light, he would ride his horn while cussing them viciously and scowling at them when they looked in their mirrors. I sat in the back, sliding from side to side on the blue vinyl-covered seat, mute and numb with terror. Between slides, I caught a glimpse of his intense darting eyes in the rearview mirror and wondered if I hadn't seen those same eyes staring back at me from some Post Office wall.

We peaked at the top of a hill. The north bay expanded out from the foot of a steep and undulating street onto which we turned. To the left was the Golden Gate, to the right, the cities of the East Bay, and two blocks back, my stomach lay writhing in the middle of the street.

"Is it much further?" I managed to gasp.

"Not much," he said curtly.

We shot down the hill, bouncing violently on the level ground which followed each perilously steep block. When we finally reached the bottom of the hill, we careened right around a corner, tires screeching and engine revving, and sped through several intersections whose lights were just tottering between yellow and red. I was seriously re-addressing my dormant relations with God when we lurched to a stop in front of the large plaza at Pier 39.

The driver grunted, then muttered something unintelligible as he pointed towards the second story of the pier's shopping center. I did not try to decipher his cryptic utterance. At that point, I didn't care where the hell we were, as long as we were stopped. I opened the door and leaped out of the cab for fear that he might think of some other place to take me and continue his demon run. My hands were shaking as I paid him his fare, which he took without thanks, then sped away on another call, nearly hitting a jaywalking pedestrian in the process. In a mute mental hysteria, I made my way across the plaza, through the pulsating throng of tourists, up some stairs to the left, and into the foyer of a noisy restaurant in the general vicinity that demon-driver had pointed.

"Hello, there!" chirped an anorexic, overly made-up blonde woman of about thirty who stood behind an oak veneered podium. "Will there be just one of you this evening?" she continued with a plastic smile and studied exuberance as she looked from me down to her reservation book then back again. Her expressions and movements were only a bit more natural than Disney's mechanized Lincoln. The only response I could muster was a flat, blank stare. Like a well-oiled machine, her features softened to a maternal expression while she maintained her practiced smile and held up her index finger.

"One... for... dinner?" she asked in the slow sing-song reserved for very young children and foreigners.

"I need a drink," I managed to sputter.

Her face then relaxed into an equally studied look of cynical understanding.

"Wife drive'n you crazy with the shoppin', huh?"

"The bar's right through there," she said without waiting for a response as she motioned me through the large open doorway to her left. As I stumbled by her, she attempted an understanding smile (the weakest in what I saw of her repertoire). Once I was safely through the doorway, she swiveled back towards the entrance, reinstated her smile of greeting focused now on the group entering from the pier, and I heard her voice trailing off, blending with the din I was moving into: "Five for dinner?"

The restaurant was busy, but there were plenty of seats at the bar. By the time I finished my first vodka tonic, I had calmed down enough to survey the social scene. The word "pathetic" cannot begin to encompass what I saw. I found myself amidst the representative low point of the term "international," which is so often applied to San Francisco. A variety of cultures from around the world were represented, dressed in nauseating regalia of fluorescent, casual, traveling clothes. They all seemed to be smiling with the dizzy exuberance of a troop of retarded monkeys. Their expressions seemed to say, "Oh gosh, really, can it be any better than this?"

Just then a woman's voice suddenly bellowed behind me, "Oh, Ned, look!"

I spun round like a cornered wildcat (knocking my third drink over in the process) expecting to find a cave woman with a spear raised and pointed at my heart. Instead, I saw a short, pudgy woman of fifty or so standing a few feet from me.

"We could see the Golden Gate Bridge and Salsaleedoe from here at these tables by the window if we ate here."

I turned to look where she was pointing as if I needed to confirm that the huge plate glass windows and the view they afforded were still there. When I looked back, she had slumped her shoulders forward in a supplicant manner and stuck her lower lip out slightly as her eyes went dewy.

"Please, can we eat here, daddy?" she turned and drawled to a rotund man only a few years her senior who stood just behind her wearing Nikes, tube socks pulled up to his knees, tan Bermuda shorts, and a Property of Alcatraz T-shirt.

"Well, Charlotte," boomed Ned, "that pretty young girl up front there said I was dressed okay, so…" he appeared to deliberate for a moment, then almost shouted: "Oh, why not!"

Charlotte nearly collapsed in a spasm of rapture as Ned turned, beaming in his fresh triumph, to go and make the appropriate reservations. The nausea I had had in the taxi seemed suddenly to overwhelm me again. I turned back to the bar where a broad-faced Hispanic bartender named Miguel (as I gleaned from his name tag) was cleaning up my spilled drink.

"My God, where do these assholes come from?" I asked just under my breath. Miguel must have heard me because he looked at me and smiled, shaking his head as though he understood exactly what I was saying.

"I've got to get to somewhere different than this," I said in a pleading tone. "Can you think of any place close that's cooler than this?"

He looked calmly at me and what I was wearing, while setting the fresh drink he had poured in front of me. "Take a cab to the Triangle," he said. "I think that'll be more what you're looking for."

His steady mien, coupled with a fleeting memory of that demon cab driver, unnerved me a bit, so I asked cautiously, "What's this place like?"

"It's not just one place; it's a few bars. You'll want to go to the Balboa Cafe."

He must have sensed my uncertainty because he looked at me with that same calm expression and said:

"Don't worry. It's a straight place. You'll like it better than here."

After sitting for a few minutes in silent deliberation, I downed my drink, slammed the empty glass on the counter, and said with a sudden burst of enthusiasm, "I thank you sincerely, Miguel, my man!"

I suddenly felt light, almost buoyant. A feeling of jovial benevolence and pity towards humanity seemed to have taken hold of me. Jumping off the stool, I threw a fifty on the bar and ambled over to a table by the window where Charlotte and Ned now sat devouring a plate of deep-fried calimari.

They both stared and blinked like cows caught unexpectedly in a spotlight when I bent down, spread my arms out over the table and put a hand on each of their shoulders. I saw their uncertainty was growing to genuine fear in spite of the fat, friendly smile I had put on for them, and that I'd need to say something to calm them pronto, or they might start shrieking and blow the feeling I was having.

"I just wanted to tell you folks," I began in the most sonorous, friendly tone I could, "that I hope you enjoy your meal with this *gorgeous* view you've got and that you have a swell time the rest of your stay here in San Francisco."

Their faces relaxed into smiles of relief and pleasure as Ned thundered, "Well, thank you! Thank you very much! That sure is nice of you. What, are you the manager here?"

"No," I said as I stood up, taking my hands off their shoulders, "but I'm thinking of buying this place, and I just want to get a jump on creating a friendly reputation."

"Oh, isn't that nice, Ned," gushed Charlotte. "Well, you'll do just fine, I'm sure."

"Oh, I feel pretty confident of that," I said, "as long as I have customers like you."

I gave her a quick wink to the side as I said this, which caused a slight tremor of alarm to pass over her fleshy face. But I continued to smile like a hayseed, and she began immediately to swoon again.

"Well, I'll leave you to enjoy your meal now," I said, taking my cue from a waitress approaching with two plates of oil-laden, fried fish.

Charlotte batted her eyes coquettishly like some demure, corpulent southern belle and asked, "Would you mind taking our picture before you go?"

"Oh, I was about to insist on you letting me," I said as I abruptly seized from her hand the camera she had pulled from her bulging purse.

Taking four vigorous steps backwards, negotiating my way through the tables behind me, I began to wave them together and shout, "Smile!" I then dropped to my knees and focused on Charlotte's enormous left breast, foregrounding the Golden Gate Bridge just to its right. I snapped off the picture, leaped up and bounded back to their table.

"Thank you so much," they shouted in unison as Charlotte took the camera.

My eyelids drooping to a sleepy half-mast, I clicked my heels together and swept my right arm to my front as I smiled and bowed slightly. With that, I pivoted round and walked by the bar straight for the exit. Miguel beckoned me to come get my change, but I waved him off like a country squire. He smirked, but then laughed and shook his head as I marched by, out through the foyer and onto the pier.

I made a beeline down the stairs and straight for the taxis waiting in front of the pier, mentally ready to seize my prize, which I felt to be almost in my grasp. I could feel her presence beckoning me on, calling me forth into the murky distance like some mythological siren. I could hear her... I could almost see her... oh, my Darling, you were there, were you not?

∼

I WOKE TO THE BRIGHT, BLURRED LIGHT OF MORNING. My eyes slowly focused on a white plastered ceiling. I raised myself on my elbows and discovered I was lying on an enormous white leather couch near a matching chair and a brushed steel coffee table in the middle of a large airy room with a high ceiling. A floor of black slate accentuated a neo-modern motif, the apparent theme of the sparsely decorated room. Two large archways stood at either end of the room, and an average-sized open doorway stood by the archway at the northwest end. Like the ceiling, the walls were of white plaster and bare except for a very large, expensively framed print of Edvard Munch's *The Scream*, which hung at eye level in front of the couch. Barren as they were, the walls glared with the light of the morning sun. When I raised myself a little further to look over the high back of the couch, my eyes encountered the direct light of that angry star, which was pouring through several large windows that faced northeast.

I fell back on the couch to allow my eyes to recover and adjust to the painful, stabbing light. My head felt packed full of cotton, and the familiar hum-buzz, always present on the morning after the night of a drunken stupor, rang low and steady in my ears. The fact that I had no idea where I was or how I had gotten there was in no way upsetting to me. I trusted my subconscious implicitly. I learned in my first few years of college that once reverted to that level of consciousness, I was probably in hands as safe as any guardian angel's. Other than an occasional bruise, my subconscious self had delivered me from harm again and again, bringing me thus to many a similar situation.

My eyes having adapted to the light, I swung my feet off the couch onto the ground and sat up. My head was spinning a bit, but I stood up anyway, knowing you can't give in to that or you'll be couch-bound all day. I walked over to the windows to have myself a look at my host's and/or hostess' view. It was a lovely panorama, though my disgruntled stomach, more unsettled by the dizzying height, lobbied with painful gurgles to step back from it. Just to the right, Alcatraz stood imposingly in the middle of the Bay, while the Golden Gate hovered over to the left. Whose ever house I was in, they had a load of money. It took no local to help me figure that out. This was an international vista, the kind they put on postcards.

As I was admiring the view, I heard a flutter of bird's wings from the other room towards the arch by the doorway. As I turned toward this sound, a slight, effeminate older man dressed in powder blue sweats emerged from the doorway and sauntered slowly to the closest archway. My surprise turned to panic when he appraised me without a word then smiled a playfully sinister, knowing smile. I glanced over to an ebony table behind the couch on which I saw my newly purchased Georgio Armani suit neatly folded. I then took note of what I was wearing: light pink sweats. The bird I assumed I had just heard let out a deafening squawk as the man disappeared through the archway, and I nearly collapsed on the floor in a trembling fit of mortification at the circumstance in which my apparently errant subconscious had placed me.

A slight clattering of dishes began to issue from the kitchen, and after a short time, I heard coffee percolating. I staggered back to the couch, hoping to find an abyss in which to throw myself, instead of the comfortable cushions onto which I fell. My hands over my eyes, I lay struggling to remember the now black-as-pitch end of the previous evening.

The image of a young, blue-eyed sympathetic blonde woman was my last and most prominent recollection. After that, there were only snippets of experiences — things that struck me for some inexplicable reason: a bright, well-furnished foyer of an apartment building; the wane, drawn face of the man I had just seen as he shut a large entry door behind me; the same white ceiling I had seen when I woke up and my voice droning on and on about something sad. That was it.

"And how's our little romantic this morning?" I heard a gravelly, contralto voice near at hand ask.

I took my hands off my eyes and saw the man setting a plate of fruit and pastries and a mug of steaming coffee on the table in front of me.

"I certainly hope we're a little more cheerful today," he said with a smile. "Your monologue kept us up late last night."

"Monologue?" I asked with a tremor. "We stayed up *talking* last night?"

"Well," he said with a playful lilt that made my stomach heave, "I imagine you expected a bit more. But I couldn't have lived with myself knowing you might not have felt so good about yourself in the morning."

This gave me little comfort. I tried to sit up to take the mug he was now holding out to me, but my head swirled and swam, forcing me to lie back down momentarily to gain strength for the endeavor. I was hopeful the caffeine might rejuvenate me, clearing my head for the energy this conversation was obviously going to take, so I forced myself up and took the cup from him. He wore the same wry, knowing smile throughout my efforts.

"Well, my little Ulysses, what a mess you were last night," he said, again in the playful tone of a lover that was so upsetting to my stomach.

"I've decided you must be after some woman, if I take the gibberish you were rambling on about last night correctly," he continued. "I know she's the love of your life and all - good God, you did go on about that! But I never managed to get a coherent answer out of you as to what makes you think you'll find her here, or anywhere for that matter? I mean, it really is absurd. I tried to tell you last night that you can't force it; you've got to let it happen on its own."

He had crossed his skinny legs, placed his elbow on his knee, and was resting his chin in the palm of his bony hand. His brow was arched in mocking inquisition, an expression which with his drawn features gave him an evil appearance.

I did not reply, but instead sat with my legs pulled up to my chest and continued sipping my coffee. I was angry at myself for having betrayed my inner feelings to this contemptuous stranger and that this was the level to which my drunken desperation had driven me. He was obviously incapable of understanding the breadth and depth of my vision, so I decided silence was the best way to deal with him.

"We're certainly less talkative today than we were last night, aren't we?" he said after a moment.

He then stood up and ambled back to the kitchen, looking

back over his shoulder to smile a sly, flirtatious smile just before he turned the corner out of sight.

Just then, the sympathetic blonde I remembered from the night before walked in the room, rubbing her eyes. When she saw me, she seemed surprised, then appeared to remember whatever there was to remember. She shuffled over to me wearing maternal concern on her pretty round face. Sitting down on the coffee table as the sarcastic old man had, she said nothing for a moment.

I felt uncomfortable with the way she was gazing at me, so I turned around to take in the view again. When I turned back, she got up and sat next to me, putting her arm on my shoulder and looking at me solicitously.

"I was really worried about you last night," she said with an unflinching sincerity that was even more unnerving. "That's why I brought you home with me. I was afraid you might, like, do something *drastic.*"

Her eyes flashed with genuine fear and uncertainty at the word "drastic," not only as though she had just then believed in the dreadful possibilities conjured up by the word, but also in surprise, as if it had been someone other than she who had said it. I felt a sudden and overwhelming sense of pity for her. She appeared so helpless, so unsure as to what to make of me. She continued to look at me searchingly, as though the features of my face might reveal some clue to a mystery about me she wished to solve.

"Who is she?" she asked timidly.

"Who is who?" I replied, turning away again as I did so.

"I don't know," she responded. "All I could figure out from what you said last night is that some woman gave you all her money and left and that you're looking for her now."

"Oh, isn't this precious."

We both turned to see the older man, wearing the same cynical expression he had earlier, leaning against the archway with a large cockatoo on his shoulder. The bird spread its wings and flapped them slowly as the man walked over and sat down on the coffee table again.

"Cherice, you'll need to be more discriminating about whom you bring home. This boy, I believe, has extreme neurotic tendencies."

He smirked at me. I turned to the girl and frowned.

"Uncle Freddie, stop it," said Cherice, though obviously suppressing a smile.

Rocking back slightly, Uncle Freddie put his hand to his chest and let his jaw drop in an effeminate gesture of offense taken, unsettling the cockatoo, who spread its wings slightly to balance itself.

"Why, Cherice, I'm shocked! Just because your father pays the rent on this place doesn't mean that you have the run of it and can bring home just any drunken reprobate you find in one of those yuppie bars you go to. Edgar and I have rights too! He was very agitated this morning when I came down, weren't you, Edgar?"

The bird let out a deafening squawk as Uncle Freddie

frowned at Cherice. She smiled, apparently in spite of herself, and shook her head like the mother of a child whose behavior she disapproves of but is still tickled by the child's pluck. Her response caused whatever pity I had been feeling for her to dissipate. I laid back down on the couch and put my forearm over my eyes.

"Don't get comfortable, my little man," said Uncle Freddie. "If I have my way, you'll be out on your ear quite soon."

"Uncle Freddie, stop it right now, and I mean it!" Cherice said, this time without the good humor I detected before.

"Well," Freddie said breathily, a slight quiver in his voice, "I can see where *I* stand around here!"

I removed my forearm from my eyes in time to see him rise indignantly and march off to the kitchen with Edgar flapping and squawking the whole way. Cherice and I exchanged uneasy glances, and then she appeared to grow nervous. She stood up and walked around the couch behind me. Picking up my neatly folded suit, she came back and held my clothes out to me.

"I think you'll need to get dressed now," she said in a way that seemed apologetic. "There's a bathroom over there off the foyer. You can change there."

I took the clothes from her, went into the bathroom and changed.

When I came out holding the sweats, Uncle Freddie (minus Edgar) was standing directly in front of me with his legs pressed close together and his arms crossed tightly across his chest. Wrathful indignation contorted his gaunt face.

"Give me my sweats and get the hell out of here, you little shit," he said through clenched teeth.

"What the hell is your problem?" I asked with no attempt to cloak my rising anger. "What the fuck did I do to you, anyway?"

"Don't you dare speak to me that way, you bastard!" he screamed in a piercing, unnatural voice. "I listened to you, you son-of-a-bitch! I sat up after Cherice went to bed and listened to you ramble on about your god-damned ridiculous love-quest. I tried to give you some comfort, and how do you treat me this morning but like the cold, calculating bastard that you are! Now get out! Get out of here, you… you… selfish little prick!"

He stepped forward and seized his sweats from me. He then made a wild, flailing gesture toward the door and ran from the room, nearly hitting Cherice, who had rushed in wearing an expression of panic and fear.

"What happened?" she cried, looking at me as if I had just drop-kicked a bunny.

"I don't know," I said helplessly. "He just went off on me."

She ran after Uncle Freddie and left me standing there stunned beyond words. After standing a minute or two more like a lobotomized dolt, I went back and sat on the couch to put my shoes on. I sat for another minute or so, trying to regain my equilibrium, which was suffering from these recent dramas, not to mention the night before. But after a little more mental grappling, I decided it best not to think about any of what had happened. I felt exhausted and needed rest. It was still relatively early in the morning and, as I had heard nothing from upstairs for the past ten minutes, I decided to beat a quiet retreat. What I needed was to hole up in my room and get a few more hours of sleep. So I left the now tomb-like house and caught a cab back to my hotel.

⁓

WHEN I WOKE, it was early afternoon. The whole experience of that morning felt like a bad dream remembered from a distant future, but still left me torpid and disinclined toward venturing back onto the trail of my Love.

Lying under the lush covers of my bed, behind the blackout curtains of my Grand Suite, I gazed absently at the flickering pictures on the muted television, mentally questioning the nature of my pursuit. Though I tried to resist thinking about him, Uncle Freddie's comments began to float up and cast ominous shadows over my plans. He'd said my search was ridiculous, and I could see why one might think that. I had not lost my capacity to reason. And yet, the belief that I could find her was still irresistible to me. Maybe others couldn't do it, I argued to myself, but I was different because I was committed. I was also motivated by the fact that I couldn't let my Darling down because, after all, she needed me so desperately. Still, I could not quash the lingering doubt that my goal might be unattainable. I eventually stopped thinking, unmuted the TV, and began surfing through the channels.

While avoiding the soaps for fear of overstimulating myself, I ran through the plethora of reruns and talk shows available for my viewing nausea. Besides this slop, there was the full-scale attack being unleashed on the consumer. A steady stream of mediocre actors attempted to convince me of my need for cough drops, cola, bathroom tissue, hair spray, cake mix, doggie snacks, kitty litter, air freshener, and various feminine hygiene products, to name only a few. Everything presented was made to appear as though, by simply purchasing said product, the consumer would achieve an unparalleled state of bliss. It was, however, the mid-afternoon commercial's wish to first train, then gainfully employ me, or to seduce me into a personal injury lawsuit that finally provoked me to throw the remote control at the TV. I decided to shower and dress, then go out for a recuperative walk.

I walked out of the Fairmont lobby and turned right, heading north toward the bay. I knew there would very likely be some nice views from the hill as the day was clear. It was also pleasantly warm, and in spite of some residual lethargy from my listless afternoon, I felt relatively peppy. My stroll lasted around an hour and a half. I walked to Russian Hill, down to North Beach, up to Coit Tower, then back through North Beach towards the Financial District. I next spent an hour or so in City Lights Books, browsing through various things I'd read before, then went next door to Vesuvio bar where I sat upstairs looking out the window at the locals, street people, and tourists passing below me. Here, as during the whole of my outing, I never stopped studying the faces of women I saw. In many of them, I thought I could see a hunger for something unnamable, some unfulfilled desire. *Couldn't she be any one of them?* I asked myself. No, I quickly answered, she would be distinguished by something elemental within her, which would show itself in a particular look or action.

Darkness began to fall, and I was starting to get drunk. Afraid of a repeat performance of the night before, I got up and went out onto the street. The setting sun was throwing its dwindling light onto scattered clouds, turning them various hues of orange and pink and purple. Behind the clouds, the sky was melting from shade to ensuing shade of blue, moving ineluctably toward blackness. I walked up to Broadway and stood on the corner. Across and down the street, neon lights over porn shops and strip clubs blazed below the sky, which continued its sublime display. I felt a melancholy permeate my being, saturating me with an overwhelming sadness. She must be, I thought. She has to exist or I'll never make it. But what can I do? Where can I go? She is so elusive. I turned away and began to walk slowly up the block. Could she have given up? Perhaps I have already lost her? Not to this corruption, from which I could possibly save her, but to eternity. These thoughts continued to percolate in my mind as I reached Chinatown, through which I headed in the general direction of my hotel.

Chinatown had an oddly calming effect on me. In spite of the noise and the clatter from the tourist shops, and the strange faces and smell of fish everywhere, there was a vibrant quality to it. Life was going on there. I began to think about everything and wondered where I'd gotten off track. But my mind was still fuzzy. When I finally reached the hotel feeling tired and hungry, I just ordered a big meal in my room, ate, and went to bed.

The next day began as inauspiciously as the one before had ended. Though I continued to roam through various parts of the City on the lookout for her, things were not going as I'd anticipated, and I was feeling frustrated. Although I hadn't expected to find my Darling easily, I thought that once I began, my search would be sustained by an unshakable sense of purpose that would propel me in a specific direction. But, in truth, I felt even more lost than before I'd started. It was as though, having been wound tight then sent spinning towards a definite goal, I had come to a premature rest, whirling in place.

For some reason, the street people I saw throughout the City made me intensely aware of this feeling. I could never walk by them, whether they were standing or sitting or laying over to the side against a wall, without looking at them. By afternoon I started giving them money. At first, I gave twenties or fifties, but this earned too much attention because they always made such a big deal thanking me that people walking by would stop and stare. I can't say why, but I didn't want any gratitude from them; in fact, even their simple thanks grated against me. So I went to the bank and withdrew several hundred dollars in five-dollar bills, to which I reduced my contributions. I would still occasionally get a too vigorous thanks, so I began to try to make more furtive deliveries. I would wait 'til they weren't looking, then toss the bill in their hat or cup and walk quickly away. This procedure seemed to work best, so I stuck with it.

At the end of the day, I realized I wanted to keep doing it but knew it might be dangerous at night dressed as I was. I decided to go to a local thrift store to buy some less conspicuous clothes, which I did late that afternoon. The next morning, I went straight to the bank to replenish my supply of fives, which I put in a beat-up backpack I got at the thrift store. I spent the whole day walking around, slipping money to anyone who had any kind of receptacle out. Because I was worried about being recognized by giving to the same person twice, I paid close attention to the faces of my beneficiaries. I covered blocks and blocks in all directions that day and then the next, and there was never a shortage of different people on the street. I also kept a close watch for anyone who might try to follow me. I saw no one but knew another day in the same general area was probably ill-advised. I decided that night to try another part of the City where I knew there would be plenty of street people: Haight-Ashbury.

～

THE NEXT MORNING BEFORE I WOKE, I had a dream. My Love, in tie-dyed rags, was traipsing along the streets of the Haight behind a well-groomed man dressed in a dark business suit who skipped ahead pied-piper-like playing a flute. She would laugh in a crazed way then mutter, "Too late, too late, you're always too late." Of course, her face was obscured from me, but that it was my Darling girl, I had no doubt. A throng of rats swarmed close at her heels, and though they all seemed to want to leap upon her and devour her, her laughter and muttering appeared to keep them at bay.

At this point, my sleep-laden eyes rolled open to my dimly lit hotel room in time to see a rat apparently defying gravity as it slowly crept across the mirror over the dresser on the wall near the end of my bed. I leaped out of bed, grabbed my bulging money clip from the nightstand and threw it at the little beast in order to stun it. But I only saw my naked reflection in the mirror when I turned on the light. My dream had apparently bled into reality.

I began dressing frantically, certain this would be a dreadful omen if I didn't treat it as a sign as to the location of my Darling. As I was heading for the door, I saw in the full-length mirror by the bathroom that I had mixed my fine Italian clothes with my thrift store purchases, but I didn't care. She was within my grasp, and I had no time for such trifles.

I had my car brought up and asked the red-vested valet who brought it to remind me how to get to Haight street. He said it was very simple. Pointing southwest, he named the various streets I would need to take to get there. He then suggested that if I were planning on parking on the street in the Haight, I might want to have the hardtop, which I'd had him take off on a whim the day before, put back on. I thanked him for the suggestion and declined, hurriedly slipping him a wad of five-dollar bills. Again, I could not be delayed by something so inconsequential. As I pulled out of the driveway, I had already forgotten all but the first street and direction he had mentioned. But I just turned on to it and headed west. Never mind with the rest. I would simply intuit my way to my Love.

After driving for a mile or so, I reached Van Ness Avenue, which I took because it was busy and wide and the name sounded vaguely familiar. Heading south, I studied each street sign at every intersection, hoping a name might jar my memory and remind me which street the valet had recommended. When I passed Market Street, I wondered if I was making a mistake as it was a large street that ran west, but I decided to continue forward. I felt the Haight must be further south than I was, and I figured I could ask for directions if I didn't run into a familiar-sounding street soon.

After a few blocks, the road jogged right, and the neighborhood changed. Paint peeled from aging buildings. Rust spots and fading colors covered late model Fords and Chevys. Taquerias and bars dotted each block and advertisements were mainly in Spanish. More homeless, with their hungry features and tattered garb, milled around on the sidewalk. It almost felt like another country, one somewhere in the Third World. As I drove on, I grew a little nervous with the attention my car was getting. I realized I probably should have waited back at the hotel while the valet put the top back on. But I was too frustrated with being lost to worry about that. When the intersecting streets (which were numbered rather than named) reached the twenties, I took a right on 22nd and began to look for a place to ask for directions.

Within a few moments, however, another issue finally eclipsed all others in importance. I had begun to feel it mounting with greater and greater urgency since I'd passed Market Street, but had thought I could hold out 'til I reached the Haight. But I could now feel my imperious bladder would be put off no longer. I cursed it as I turned onto a street called Valencia and began an anxious search for a place to relieve myself. After a couple of blocks, I spotted a gas station. At least I could kill two birds with one stone. I pulled in and got out of my car with cautious haste, fearful of any embarrassing accident I might cause in disregard for my brimful state. I noticed five Latino men standing by a wall near where I'd parked, laughing as they watched me taking quick, ginger steps toward the bathroom. Dressed in T-shirts with rock band emblems, worn denim, and tennis shoes, they appeared harmless enough, so I just smiled good-naturedly and nodded on my way to the men's room door.

Of course, the door was locked. I then saw the sign on the door saying a key could be had at the mini-market counter inside. As I turned abruptly to rush into the store, I saw that the rebuff I'd received had caused no small amount of mirth in my audience by the wall. I smiled and shrugged my shoulders in affable resignation while hurrying around the corner to the mini-market door. A large Indian man who stood imposingly behind the counter scrutinized me with curiosity and suspicion as I rushed into the store.

"Hi, um, could I have the key to the bathroom, please?" I asked, wincing with pain from my bulging bladder.

"Xcooz me, zer, but are yoo pearabs a gustamer?" he inquired with a condescending, deferential smile. To my pained quizzical expression, he responded by pointing to a sign on the wall behind the counter which read, "Restrooms for Customer **ONLY.**"

"Give me some of those," I said through clenched teeth while pointing to condom packets hanging below the sign.

"Veery good, zer!" he said with enthusiasm, snapping several of the packages from the wall, then ringing them up on the cash register.

"Now," he asked cheerfully, "wheel there be anyting elles?"

"No," I screamed, throwing a fifty dollar bill at him, "Keep the God damned change and give me the fucking bathroom key!"

"Oooh, yehz zer!"

He slid the key across the counter to me, which I seized, then rushed out the door to the restroom, where I found my long-sought relief. I came out of the bathroom — wearing the slight, contented smile of a man who has received satisfaction — and immediately sensed that something was wrong. I looked to the wall and observed that my merry Latino compatriots had departed; but I knew something else was missing that I could not put the accusatory finger on.

It wasn't until after I had taken the key back to that capitalistic counter-tender and had walked outside that I realized with a hot flash and a sickness in the pit of my stomach what was wrong: my Black Beauty was gone. I thrust my hands in my pockets, but felt no keys. In my mind's eye I saw them dangling cheerily in the ignition. I could not contain my frustration and grief. I let out a howl of self-loathing and bitterness at the fate that had sent me in search of my Love and was now bandying me about as carelessly as a cat does a captured mouse.

All around me, people stopped what they were doing to observe the source of this unnatural shriek in the middle of their day. But most of them promptly resumed their chosen course. A few continued to stare at me with curiosity; for the rest, my suffering had been only a momentary distraction from their various individual goals. This indifference was nearly too much for me to bear, and I almost broke into tears. I did not know what to do. The thought of having to deal with the police and all their tedious questions was offensive to me. And this would further delay me in finding my Darling, who was, after all, still waiting for me to rescue her. In the end, I left my loss where it had occurred and slouched off toward the hill to the west, numb and cold in the springtime sun.

~

AFTER SHUFFLING A FEW BLOCKS WEST in dejected silence, I reached a park. The sun had risen sufficiently to give warmth to the people out on the grass and paths. I had been walking slowly, and when I neared the park's center, I stopped completely. I found myself mesmerized by the behavior of a silver-haired old woman in a pink and white cloth overcoat walking a bloated white poodle. She plodded along, and the dog dawdled behind, sniffing too long at a tree or a clump of dog shit, forcing her to give a sharp yank at the leash. I could not stop myself from watching. She and her dog soon drew near a diminutive old man who sat brooding on a green park bench. He wore wingtip shoes, a faded pair of dark wool pants, a dingy white collar shirt, and a shabby tweed sport coat. His aging brown fedora dully reflected the mid-morning sun. He had a cane on which he folded his hands and rested his chin. His blank stare betrayed an idle mind that gave no indication of ever tripping back into gear. He seemed to be sitting in wait of the final stall. I noticed that neither observed the other, though they were close enough to have taken a step forward and touched hands.

My gaze rose to the blank blue sky at which I stared for I do not know how long. Eventually, my eyes fell to a playground on the other side of the park. There, small children were scampering to and fro from the slide to the swings to the jungle gym, screeching with zeal in pursuit of the moment. Their screams seemed to grow more strident as I watched. Each shriek felt as if it were piercing my soul. Suddenly, I heard a sharp, high-pitched bark. I looked over to see the old woman holding her poodle back as it pulled passionately at the end of its leash.

"Stavy! Gustave, stop that this instant!" hollered the old woman. She was glaring down at the dog, which was scrapping its nails furiously on the pathway trying for some inexplicable reason to get at me.

I recoiled and ran off to escape the havoc this riot was making in my head.

"He won't hurt you," I heard her cry out behind me, "he just likes making a scene."

Church Street bordered the park on the west. I stopped there and wrung my hands like some overwrought silent movie character. I surveyed the hill I had been planning to climb and realized it was much steeper than it appeared from a distance. Though it was only a block long, I decided I was in no mood to play the mountaineer. Gustave had stopped barking, but the screams of the children were still upsetting me. I turned and headed south on Church to put the racket they were making completely out of earshot. I decided I could walk around the hill, then go west again once a less arduous way presented itself.

Several blocks on, I came to a street with a variety of markets, cafés, coffeehouses, and shops. It was nearing eleven or so in the morning, and I hadn't had anything to eat. I was also tired from recent travails and decided some caffeine might help my cause as well. I walked up the street and soon found a place that was nearly empty.

A young woman with a nose ring and cropped hair dyed Donny Osmond purple stood behind a counter with her arms folded across her chest regarding me with a sort of hostile indifference. A black turtleneck sweater clung to her thin upper torso and, as I made my way up to the counter to scan the menu, a short red and black plaid skirt covering her disproportionately large hips came into view. Black leotards hugged her legs, which narrowed into tiny feet concealed in black, thick-soled shoes.

Hardly in the best of spirits myself, I still tried smiling to see if I could win her over. She frowned then turned her back to me, busying herself behind the counter. She kept her back to me for a minute or so, cleaning this and organizing that. When she turned around, I dared to hazard an order of coffee and a croissant. With thinly veiled disdain, she came over, took my money, then slid my order across the counter to me, turning away abruptly in response to my thanks. I lingered, doctoring my coffee at the counter. She finally turned around again, and I threw several dollars in the tip jar, smiling at her one more time.

"Oh, thank you so much," she said, breaking into a mock Southern accent, "I've always depended on the kindness of strange men."

A sultry young woman with long chestnut hair and brown eyes sitting at a nearby table let out a husky chuckle.

"Yes, I'm sure I do appear strange to you, don't I?" I responded with unmasked condescension. "But then anyone in pursuit of a higher cause always appears strange to the common people."

"Oh," she said with a smirk, "I should have figured you for a whacked religious type by your duds. What, are you, a wayward Mormon or something?"

The sultry blonde laughed outright.

"No, my dear, *your* soul is not the goal of my quest," I said with cool dignity, "and I'm sure you would never understand what it is I *am* searching for, so I won't bother trying to explain myself to you."

In an instant, her hand shot across the counter and grabbed my shirt. She then yanked me forward and said:

"Let's get one thing fucking straight right now, buddy boy: I am not your or any other fucking man's 'dear.' You got that?"

The expression on her face seemed to suggest she was prepared to eviscerate the lungs of yours truly if I did not agree with her.

"I apologize if anything I said was offensive to you."

She let go of my shirt, and I rocked back on the balls of my feet like a round-bottomed, blow-up punching clown. She was still glaring at me as I made my way over to a table in the corner by the front window. When I finished my coffee and pastry, I didn't feel up to continuing my quest just then, so I went up and ordered a beer. Though the purple-haired girl remained somewhat surly, the beer was delivered without incident.

While I was waiting for my second cerveza, I saw that the sultry blonde was observing me with what appeared to be a smile. I assumed she was still laughing at me, so I just ignored her. I went back to my table where I sat and stared out the window for the next half hour or so. I knew I should be on the move toward my Dearest, that she might very well have been escaping me as I sat there idling. But I did not care. I felt tired and bitter toward her for leading me into these circumstances. I even imagined that just then she might also be suffering like me, and I actually enjoyed the thought. Suddenly, the sultry blonde set a beer down in front of me and took a seat at my table.

"This is for you," she said. "I hope you don't mind. I'm interested in what you said when you first came in."

I must have looked surprised because she smiled at me reassuringly. I looked over at the purple-haired girl. She appeared very similar to when I had first come in, except that her face was now contorted into a hostile scowl directed at me. I picked up the beer and took an extended swig, finishing nearly half the bottle in a single gulp.

"What did you mean when you said you were in pursuit of a higher goal?"

She seemed sincere, but I was uncertain about whether or not to answer her. I finally decided I was feeling so down that it was worth the risk of talking to her just to get rid of the negative feelings I was having. Maybe, I speculated, they were thwarting my intuition and causing all my recent woes.

"I am looking for someone," I replied, watching the half-empty beer bottle I was slowly rotating in the palm of my hand. "Someone… very important."

"But what did you mean by a higher goal if you're looking for a person?" she asked, again with apparent sincerity.

An amused, quizzical expression played on her face. She couldn't have been more than twenty-two. She had seemed sultry before, but now she appeared almost innocent, even angelic. I was distracted just then by the motion of the purple-haired girl on the other side of the café. She was trying to appear as though she was straightening things out, moving newspapers and repositioning chairs. But it was obvious she was interested, even annoyed, that the blonde was sitting with me.

"So what about it?"

"I... am searching for my soul mate," I rejoined after a pause.

"Aren't we all," she wryly stated. "But what does that have to do with all this higher cause stuff?"

"Because she is waiting for me to save her even as we speak. She needs me to find her and rescue her from this sickening, pathetic life so that we can create a higher reality together through our Love."

"I don't get it," she said. "By the way you're talking, it sounds like you don't even know her. Like, how do you think you're going to find this one particular woman? I mean, don't you know you can't force that kind of thing?"

"But you don't understand," I cried with sudden passion as I leaned across the table. "I *will* find her, because it is *our* fate!"

"You'll never find anybody," came a vicious voice from nearby.

Both the blonde and I turned to the purple-haired girl who stood a few feet away with a bitter, savage expression etched on her face.

"She's a construct of the male's female ideal based on false conception of gender roles that can be traced all the way back to the dawn of Western (she raised her hands and used two fingers to indicate the insertion of quotes) civilization."

"Oh, Mimi, please," groaned the blonde, "don't start preaching, he was just…"

"You just shut up," she snapped. "I can't believe you're sitting here with this asshole listening to all his male domineering bullshit about saving some woman who doesn't need him or any other man to save her."

A full minute of silence followed this statement, during which the two of them glared at each other. I was trying to think of a way to crawl away unnoticed or at least unhindered, but I was at a loss as to how to break this stalemate tactfully. My bladder (the unexpected guide of my activities that morning) then reminded me of the coffee and beers I had drunk, suggesting a potential out.

"Ah, excuse me," I ventured, "but is there a bathroom I could use?"

They turned in unison as though they were about to leap on me, but the purple-haired girl just pointed authoritatively to a door behind the counter without saying anything. I got up and went to the bathroom, which was on the left down a dimly lit hall.

It was a pretty small, straightforward bathroom (white sink, white commode, graffiti-less white walls, and a mirror), so there wasn't much to entertain myself with while I waited for things to cool down out there. I took note of the wear and tear on my face in the mirror: dark circles, sunken eyes, and a sick, almost ghostly pale complexion. I knew my uneven lifestyle was the main cause. I determined I'd better start taking better care of myself. I had to be able to make that oh-so-necessary good first impression on my Darling. It would be hard enough to combat her well-worn cynicism, let alone deal with an initial physical repulsion. Just then, I noticed in the mirror that the door, which I had failed to lock, was opening slowly.

"Ah, somebody's in here," I said loud enough to be heard outside the door.

"I know," I heard the blonde say as she pushed her way in and shut the door.

Before I had a chance to respond, she was on me: kissing me, groping me, then sticking her hand down my pants. I struggled with her initially, but after a minute or so, I stopped resisting and let her have her way with me. She quickly unzipped my pants and dropped to her knees. She then took me in hand and began to use her mouth in a way I could not help but enjoy. For how long this went on, I could not have said, but several minutes must have passed. When the bathroom door creaked, I opened my eyes to see the purple-haired girl standing in front of me, a horrified expression on her face.

"You bitch," I heard her whisper. Then she screamed, "You fucking bitch!"

The blonde stood up, turned to her and said, "I just wanted you to know that just because I slept with you, doesn't mean you own me. I can and will do what I feel like doing, and don't you forget it."

With that she pushed her way past the purple-haired girl, who stood dumbstruck in the doorway. I scrambled to get my pants up from my knees, then zipped them up with hasty caution to avoid accidentally snaring myself. The purple-haired girl stood there staring at me blankly. I didn't know what to do. I was afraid she might attack me if I tried to push past her like the blonde had, so I decided to wait for her to leave. Her gaze soon gained a spiteful focus.

"I'll tell you what I'd like to do," she said, her voice low and sinister. "I'd like to put your balls in a meat grinder. I don't know what's going to happen to you, but I hope you come to a very *bad* end."

She paused, her expression growing even more malevolent, then said , "I only wish I had the balls to stop you right now."

We looked at each other a moment longer, me cowering and her glowering, until she walked off down the hall out to the café. I followed her after a minute, creeping up to the door and opening it slightly to survey the scene. I saw the purple-haired girl behind the counter, again moving from here to there, perfunctorily cleaning and ordering things. I could not see whether the blonde was still there.

Pushing the door open, I hustled past the counter, not venturing a look in that direction. But I was shocked almost to a standstill when I saw the blonde sitting where she'd been sitting before. She smiled and winked when she saw me. I put my head down and hurried out the front door without looking back. I was so agitated and confused I ran headlong several blocks before I finally had to stop to catch my breath. As I stooped with hands on knees, heaving air in and out, I kept glancing back to make sure that girl hadn't acquired "the balls" she'd wished for and was now coming after me with a finely sharpened deli knife.

"Ned! Look!" I heard a familiar voice screech from close by. "It's that young man whose going to buy that Pier we went to!"

I looked up to see Ned and Charlotte sitting in front of me in an open-air "motorized cable car." She was pointing at me, and both of them were busting their faces with ecstatic grins. When they saw I recognized them, they both waved in unison. As they pulled away, Ned trumpeted out:

"We sure are hav'n a swell time, just like you wished we would!"

I waved back mechanically and even managed a faint smile. But as I watched them go over a hill out of sight, I felt a sudden loathing for those two fat, flat-footed morons. I walked over to a nearby phone booth and called a taxi. It was late afternoon, and I had had enough. Even if that woman I was looking for was still in the Haight where my dream had placed her, I did not care. When the taxi arrived, I went back to my suite and curled up under the heavy covers, shivering nonetheless until sleep crept over me like death.

∼

THE TWITTER OF THE TELEPHONE seeped into my dreams and woke me. I rolled over. The clock read 3:00 A.M. Cursing and fumbling for the phone in the dark, I finally knocked it off the nightstand onto the floor.

"Mr. Askew!... Mr. Askew?" I heard someone cry out from the castaway receiver.

I groped around and finally touched the cord, which I yanked 'til the phone was in hand.

"Yeah, what is it?"

"I'm terribly sorry, Mr. Askew, but there's a police officer on the line who wants to speak with you."

A hot flash shot through my still sleep-numbed body. I turned on the light and sat bolt upright in bed. In the following moment of silence, I scoured my memory for anything I might have done in the last few days that could have been illegal. Myriad possibilities came to mind.

"Mr. Askew... are you there?"

"Yes, yes, " I answered, trying not to sound guilty of anything.

"Well, I am truly sorry, Mr. Askew, but this officer has been terribly persistent," said the clerk. "He absolutely insists on speaking with you."

"Yes," I responded, trying again to sound calm and assured. "Of course, I'll be happy to speak with the officer."

"Very well, sir. I'll patch him through to your room."

"Ah, excuse me," I said quickly, "I didn't get your name?"

"It's James, sir," he said with enthusiasm.

"James, yes, I see, um..." I panicked with how to ask him what it was about.

"Was there something else you need, sir?"

"Ah, yes, James, I'd... ah, I'd like, um, I'd like a bottle of champagne sent up to my room. Can you arrange that?"

"Why certainly, Mr. Askew!" he bubbled in anticipation of the order. "Will there be anything else, sir?"

"No," I said, disappointed with myself, "that'll do, James."

"Very well, sir," he said. "I'll put the officer through to your room now."

I turned on the bedside lamp and sat only a moment before the phone warbled again. I stared at it as it rang. Perhaps this would be the end of my quest. The thought of having wasted the opportunity of finding my Love the previous day made me sick. How could I have been so faint of heart? My Darling had come to me in a dream, offered herself up to me, and I, lazy oaf that I was, had given up pursuing her when I was so close. Now it appeared I was to be thwarted by fate, losing my freedom to find her through some petty infraction of social decorum. I finally reached for the phone, stretching forth as if to pull the lever to release the blade of a guillotine in which my head was blocked.

"Yes," I said.

"Is this Mr. Spencer Askew?" I heard a gruff, authoritative voice demand.

"Yes."

"Mr. Askew, this is Sergeant Mulhany from the San Francisco Police Department. I have a few questions I need to ask you."

"So I've been informed, Sergeant Mulhany, please proceed." I decided I wanted to get right to business.

"Mr. Askew, do you know a Jesus Alverez?" the Sergeant asked.

This question did not alarm me as much as others might have, though I still could not imagine where in the hell it might lead. I decide to be evasive.

"I know many people, Sergeant Mulhany."

"Well, I'm asking if you know one named Jesus Alverez, Mr. Askew," the Sergeant said with unmasked irritation.

"The result of knowing many people, Sergeant, is that one sometimes forgets names. It is entirely possible that I know a person with such a name but have forgotten their name and remember only their face."

"Mr. Askew, may I ask if you own a vehicle?"

"Yes, I do."

I answered before thinking, and for some reason, regretted doing so immediately.

"Well, may I ask if you know where that vehicle is?" he asked, a cool edge to his tone.

In a flash, I understood the situation. They had nabbed one of those guys who'd taken my Black Beauty. In my difficulties, I had completely forgotten it was gone. Now I saw a person's life was held in the balance based on this thing I had so easily forgotten. Even though I wanted the car back, I couldn't stomach the thought of him burning for something so insignificant.

"Oh my God!" I shouted. "You're holding Jesus!"

"Now you're getting the picture, aren't you, Mr. Askew?"

"Well, you've got to release him," I yelled. "It was a misunderstanding between him and me, I'm sure. He must have thought I wanted him to keep the car overnight. It was a simple communication problem."

"Just what were you having Mr. Alverez do for you, Mr. Askew?" the Sergeant asked suspiciously.

My mind went blank.

"Ah, he, ah," I stuttered, groping for something, anything to say; then I came up with it, "he was supposed to wash and wax it."

I took a breath, crossed my fingers and hoped that somehow, some way, this guy Jesus had had the same idea.

Another pause. I began to perspire.

"Okay," Sergeant Mulhany said with obvious disappointment, "that's what he said he was doing."

I felt as if I had won a prize. I almost shouted with joy, but I checked myself. I knew there could be further complications if I didn't play it cool.

"Are you going to release him?" I ventured after a moment.

"Well, if what you're saying is true, Mr. Askew, we have no reason to hold him, do we? We'll just let him go… with your car."

"Ah, well," I stammered again in confusion, "maybe you should wait until I come down… so I can talk to Jesus and clear things up with him."

"I'll have to tell him you want him to wait for you," he said sharply. "We can't hold someone who hasn't done anything wrong, Mr. Askew."

"All right, fine, I'll be right down," I said, then hung up the phone.

I began dressing frantically. I was worried Jesus might take advantage of my benevolence and take off again in my Black Beauty if I didn't get down there before the cogs of the police bureaucracy had turned enough to spit him out. Obviously, this would make things difficult as the police would not likely be sympathetic to my plight.

I rushed out the door and ran into the steward bringing the champagne I had ordered. Stabbing my hand in my pocket, I came up with another wad of fives.

"Take that and the wine and go have yourself some fun," I said to brush him off.

I then rushed into the waiting elevator.

"Thanks... I know just the boy," he announced, winking as the doors closed in front of me. I had no time even to feel appropriately sickened by this.

I caught a cab to the police station and went to the information desk where I found out that Jesus had been released. My car, however, had not. Evidently, Sergeant Mulhany had been having his little fun with me. The car had been impounded because Jesus was unable to prove it was his. It could not be released for another five hours, at nine in the morning.

"Did Jesus leave any kind of message for me?" I asked the clerk, just out of curiosity.

"No," replied the clerk, who began immediately to act as though I was not there. I decided not to ask anything else. I figured it best to drop the whole thing and consider myself lucky that something worse hadn't come of it.

I walked out of the station and stood at the curb, looking across the streets at the shimmering signs of the bail bondsmen. The pink and blue of the neon glowed garishly. Below the signs, the stark, white light from the offices of the bondsmen shot out onto the street, offering their blunt, unrepentantly temporary redemption. But they had nothing to offer me.

I walked up to the corner to hail a cab. But then the idea of going back to my hotel room did not appeal to me for some reason, so I spent the next few hours hanging around the station. I figured I'd just wait to pick up my car. It wasn't long, though, before I got tired of watching the dregs of society swirl through the waiting room. When I looked at the various worn and weary faces, their stories ballooned up before my eyes. With each person, I saw living rooms cluttered with yard sale furniture and poorly painted landscapes; bedrooms with unmade beds and clothes strewn over broken-down dressers and pile-carpeted floors.

I went out on the street and started walking without purpose or aim. I avoided the eyes of people I saw. I thought nothing. I felt nothing.

Finally, 9:00 A.M. came. I went back to the station and began the long process of getting my car released. After waiting in line for an hour, I realized I didn't have any ID. I was too tired to even be angry. I just caught a cab back to the hotel. When I got back to my room, I was so exhausted I fell onto the bed and slept for several hours.

I woke around two in the afternoon, my head clouded with another dream about my Darling. She was cloaked in an ethereal fog through which she was wandering. Though I could not see her clearly, I was close to her. But she was unaware of me. I tried calling out to her; she could not hear me. I began to chase her, but she drifted away, growing murkier in the fog. I felt she was carried away against her will, that she wanted me to find her, but that she could not help moving away. Then I woke up.

A sense of longing and dread took hold of me. I felt weak, then angry with that weakness. I am a fool, I thought. She is going away from me now, I can feel it, and I sleep like the imbecile that I am. I don't deserve her. How could someone like her want me, a person so enfeebled in body and spirit? But, oh, I need her! I need her strength to carry on. How can I face this life alone, without her? No! I can't, and I won't! I will break that force that pulls her away from me. I will pursue her to the ends of the Earth, if only to savor for a moment the bliss that our love will be.

I hurried back to the station, waited in line for three hours, and got my car. Back at the hotel, I showered, dressed, and headed out on the town, sure that I could not fail to find my Love that very night.

~

THE EVENING DID NOT GO WELL. I bounced from bar to bar, not meeting anyone, let alone my Love. I stuck it out until around midnight, but I finally ended up alone by the water near the Bay Bridge. I was depressed but still struck by the beauty before me. The golden lights from cities shimmered across the bay; they flickered and skipped on the water which lapped up to the sea wall at my feet. The bridge itself rose from the water in majestic splendor. Its drab gray daytime countenance was transformed at night by glowing ivory lights draped like a string of pearls across its towers. The poignancy of the moment overwhelmed me. I was, after all, enjoying this enchanting scene without my Love. I knew that any beauty I observed would always be sullied if she was not with me, sharing the moment. And right then, she seemed completely unattainable. I hung my head, and the water seemed to call to me.

I had decided to throw myself in when a brightly-lit bar teeming with people caught my eye. Well, I thought, if I am going to end it all — especially in this icy cold bay — I want at least to numb myself beforehand by getting shitfaced drunk. So I crossed the street and went into the bar.

Upon entering, I scanned the room. The yuppies were out in full force, checking each other out to see who had more of what and who could out-do the other. They all appeared indifferent to me, but I knew they were secretly sizing me up as well. A multitude of beautiful women were there, but they all seemed so unalluringly luring. They had their physical beauty, to be sure, but what would there be once I'd torn through their façade with a few simple questions about life and beauty? It wasn't even worth the effort. Besides, I knew my Darling would never come to a place such as the high-ceilinged, cacophonous nightmare in which I stood. I began to push my way through the crowd toward the bar for my last drunken spree.

After around five minutes of maneuvering through the throng, I finally found a space at the bar. Five more minutes were spent trying to get the bartender's attention. I finally succeeded in ordering and receiving a double vodka tonic, and I tipped him liberally so that nothing would impede the drunk I was after. At the sight of the hundred I slid him, he became peppy and enthusiastically promised to remember me.

I drank slowly, trying to draw up the necessary strength for my foray into that unknown darkness of death. Of course, I felt sorry for myself, but I felt a deep and unabiding pity for my Love. After all, I had conceived of her and had thus experienced at least the pleasure of knowing what could have been. But she — my poor Dear — had lost me before knowing even the potential sweet fruit of our love. It was so sad to think of — nearly unbearable. I ordered another double.

I drank indifferent to all around me for awhile, until my reverie was disturbed by a man with the thick-browed, phlegmatic look of an Eastern European muscling his way up next to me. He called out to the bartender, who took his order, then brought the drink. His brow was furrowed, and his mood seemed morose. He looked at no one in particular as he drank but instead gazed absently around the bar. Occasionally, he winced in apparent pain or confusion, then muttered under his breath as though he was mulling something over in his mind. After a minute or two, he turned to me as though he had just realized I was there and stared straight into my eyes.

"Why?" he implored.

He spoke clearly, but I detected an accent.

"What?"

"How can it be?" he continued. "Was that not wrong? Was that not very wrong?"

I looked behind me to see if there was someone else to whom he was talking. A suit back faced me. When I turned back, he was regarding me in the same way.

"You are obviously American, so how can that have happened? How can she have done such a thing to me, another human being?" he demanded without malice or anger, but with a sort of self-pity.

"I... I... I don't know."

"But you should know," he insisted. "You *should* know."

He downed his drink, then ordered another before turning to me again. Instead of calming him, the drink animated him further. He looked as though he was going to grab me by the shoulders and shake me. But when he finally spoke, his voice sounded strangely calm.

"Before I come to your country," he began — and I was now certain his was a Russian accent. "I study your history and your literature. I watch television. I see movies. I prepare myself in this way. Then I come to your country and I want to make something of myself. I get a job here and try to fit in. I do this by coming out to bars to meet people. It has been a pretty lonely time for me. Everybody seems to want to talk, but when they do, nothing ever happens. Americans are hard to become friends with, I have found."

He paused, looked away from me, and took a healthy pull at his drink.

"Then, tonight," he continued looking back into my eyes eagerly, "I decide it is going to be different. I decide I am going to meet someone, a person maybe to be a friend with or... who knows... but I feel I must meet someone with whom I will have something. So I come to this place and begin looking around for this someone. I am not here a long time before this woman, a very beautiful woman, comes up and starts talking to me."

Again he stopped, finishing off his drink. To my surprise, I found I was waiting for him to go on with his story.

"She had long black hair and dark blue eyes. And she was intelligent. I could tell this by the way she had of looking at other people and the comments she would make about them. She made me laugh with the things she said. I began to feel I was liking her. She was beautiful and funny, but she was sad too. She tried to pretend that she wasn't, but she was sad. I thought this may be it, maybe this could be what I've been looking for."

At these last few sentences, I felt my body grow tense. But I checked myself. I could not hope that it might be *her*. I decided to remain calm and just listen.

"And so we talk. I even make her laugh. But I notice — or maybe it is now that I notice — there is something about her, like she knows something and is keeping it from me. I remember now that she never said anything about herself. But then it did not matter. I was talking to a lovely woman after so much loneliness. I did not want to question. After an hour or so, she says that we should go to her place for drinks. So I thought, 'Finally it is happening, and with such a beautiful one too.'"

An anxiety was growing in me, drawing me toward where I felt sure he was leading. I finished my drink in one gulp in an attempt to cauterize my fraying nerves.

"When we arrive at her place, an expensive hotel, she began to be very sexy, saying very little, but looking at me in a way that told me much. I have said she was very beautiful, so of course, I went along with her. Well, we end up in bed together, and she is acting very passionate. But I can feel that something is wrong, that she is not sincere. Finally, we are laying there together, but without touching, and she says, 'You will have to go now.' Just like that, no emotion, like I was some dog she was through petting."

My head was swimming; I grew more and more sure it was my Darling as he spoke. At his last line, I could contain myself no longer: I struck the bar with a closed fist, causing a brief silence among people near us. The Russian looked at me with surprise. I was distraught, and my face had to have shown it because he seemed touched by my expression.

"My friend," he said with a quivering voice, "you truly care what has happened to me?"

"Care," I almost screamed. "My whole fucking life depends on it! Tell me the rest, now!"

"It is so good to find someone who really cares for me," he said with moistening eyes. "I am Anotole, my friend, and I want to buy you a drink first."

"Fuck the drink, tell me what happened with her," I said abruptly, causing his emerging smile to collapse into a frown.

"You will not let me buy you a drink?" he said, appearing offended.

"No, no, that's not what I meant," I said quickly. He was my link to her now, and I knew I had better treat him with kid-gloves.

"I thank you for your offer," I said, trying to appear calm. "It's just that I feel so bad for you I want to hear what happened, and then I'd be happy to take a drink from you."

This answer seemed to appeased him. With enormous effort, I maintained my composure as he finished the rest of his story.

"Well," he continued, "there is not much to tell. We stood up and began to dress in silence. She finished before me and mixed herself a drink. I cannot say why, but as I was tying my shoes, I felt more sorry for her than for myself. But together, I thought we were the saddest thing I could think of. Anyway, when I stood up, she was there by me. She put her hand to my back and gently pushed me towards the door, which she opened and pressed me through. But before she shut the door, I asked, 'Why? Why must it be like this?' She did not say anything for a moment; then she asked if I was an American citizen. I was confused by this question, but I answered that I wasn't yet. She said, 'If you become an American, you might be able to understand, but now it would be pointless to talk about.' Then she closed the door.

"I stood there for a long time feeling sick in my stomach. I could not understand it. It made no sense to me why she would act this way. She needed someone as much as I did, but she would not have a person that wanted her. It made me crazy. But here, you don't look good my friend. Let me get you that drink now."

I could hardly believe what I'd just heard. I looked with reverence at this man standing next to me. Like the burning bush in *The Ten Commandments*, he seemed to radiate a glowing light.

"Can you tell me?" I asked breathlessly as he turned to give me the drink he had gotten me.

"What, my friend?" he said smiling calmly. "What do you want me to tell you?"

"Where… where was she?"

"Oh, she was staying at some big hotel on that hill which is called Nob," he answered as he turned away to take a drink.

I cringed. Then, hesitantly, oh so trepidatiously, I asked, afraid to hear the cruel answer I knew fate had in store for me:

"What is the name of that hotel?"

"I believe…" he said, looking up to the skylight and wrinkling his brow in reflection. "I believe it is called 'Fairmont.'"

I had suspected the answer, but not its effect on me. His words landed like a solid right from Mike Tyson. My legs went limp. My head swam, and my consciousness waned. I fell forward onto the bar, backward into the backs of those around me, and then began wilting down to the small amount of ground allotted me. On my way down I glanced up to the Russian, who betrayed no panic when he realized I was in full-scale collapse. Rather, in a split second, he reached out and grabbed my shirt like the scruff of a puppy's neck, pulling me back up to the bar. He did this deftly in one fluid motion, as though he had done it many times before.

"Bartender!" he shouted. "A glass of water for my friend, please."

"I did not realize you had had so much to drink," he said after a moment of smiling at me slyly. "This makes me like you all the more, because I have found that, though Americans have a reputation for drinking, they don't hold their liquor so well as you have shown you can. I am not easily fooled. We know how to drink where I am from and you could drink with us, I am sure."

I smiled weakly, nodding at him without reply. In truth, this was all I could manage, but he appeared pleased by this response, and we stood without speaking for some moments.

Gradually, as my initial shock wore off, I regained my senses. A sense of elation grew in me as I realized my Darling was alive and near. It was almost too much to believe. Up 'til then I had had only faith to sustain me; an unsubstantiated belief that she existed because she had to in order to manifest our perfect love. This lack of sustenance had caused my recent flagging doubts. Now, however, I saw that fate — cruel though it was — had at least seen fit to validate my pursuit by delivering this harbinger of my Love's existence. I felt a power surging through me which I had never known: the lucid exhilaration of vindicated blind conviction.

I looked over to the Russian and saw that he was deep in thought. He looked gloomy and querulous, his frown and troubled brow having returned. He had ordered another drink in the interim and was near finishing it. These signs looked negative; still, I had to try and get more information from him about my Darling. He might remember her room number or possibly tell me more about what she looked like.

"Friend..." I said putting my hand on his back.

"And now she is leaving," he said heavily, slurring the words slightly as he sloughed my hand off his back. "The beautiful, sad American woman is leaving."

"What are you talking about?" I said, riveted in fear. "What do you mean leaving? Where is she going?"

"How could I know?" he said with annoyance. "Did I not tell you that she told me nothing of herself and that she kicked me out like a dog?"

"But if she told you nothing, how do you know she is leaving?"

"Do you think I am stupid?" he asked, turning to me, his face drooping in smug contempt. "Just because a woman treats me like a dog does not mean I cannot observe things."

"What did you 'observe?'" I asked curtly, impatient with his attitude and accent, which had become more pronounced as the liquor took hold.

"Her luggage bags!" he shouted at me with sudden fury.

"Her luggage bags were packed! I saw them by the door as she kicked me out!"

As he finished this sentence, which had sprayed me with spit, silence floated down from the ceiling like a billowing parachute and covered the crowd which surrounded us. I felt hundreds of eyes staring at me and my comrade. In slow motion, the hedonistic congregation parted. Two stocky, ape-like young men with butch hair cuts and sheen suits emerged from the parting. Without a word, they grasped the Russian and myself, dragged us through the bar and deposited us at the foot of the stairs outside.

"Well, that is that," said the Russian, who stood up and began brushing himself off before the bouncers were halfway up the stairs. "Where do we go now, friend?"

I looked up and was amazed to find him standing above me, smiling affably with his hand extended. I found his mood swings wild and a little frightening. But I still took his hand, and he hauled me up roughly, nearly pulling my arm out of the socket. We stood there for a moment saying nothing. He just smiled and nodded his head stupidly.

"Show me the room the woman you met was in," I blurted out.

He frowned.

"Why can we not just forget this woman?" he asked sharply. "We are friends now. We can meet other women."

"You don't understand," I declared. "I'm not interested in other women. I must find the woman you met! *She* is the only woman I will ever be interested in."

"Do you know her?" he demanded, regarding me suspiciously. "How could you know her?"

Then his features softened, and he said in a wounded voice:

"We are friends now, anyway. What difference does one woman or another make?"

Like two circling predators, we studied each other for a weakness. Both of our souls were hungry. Both of us were searching for relief. But, though we shared these feelings, my need was stronger. I sensed the Russian saw this too but was resisting admitting it.

"What was her room number?" I repeated.

Again we stood staring at each other, saying nothing. Suddenly, the Russian appeared to weaken. His lower lip quivered slightly. He began to shake his head and looked as if he was going to cry. I fought feeling sorry for him, because I could not waiver. My salvation was close at hand, and I could not sacrifice it for anyone, not even the messenger of that salvation.

After a few more moments, he stood up to his full height and his features became bitter and hard as he glared down at me. I could see his pride had reared its head and would allow him to say nothing more. So I turned my back on him and went to hail a taxi. One soon came by, and as I was getting in, I saw the Russian standing where I had left him, still glaring at me with hateful eyes. I gave the driver a fifty and told him to get me to the Fairmont as fast as he could.

Searching for Her

~

I RUSHED TO THE FRONT DESK when I got to the hotel and called a clerk aside to ask if a woman fitting the Russian's description had checked out in the last two hours. My bill was running well over fifteen thousand and this clerk must have known it, because he seemed uncertain about whether or not to give me the information. I had about five hundred dollars in my pocket, of which I gave him two to help loosen his morals. He motioned me to follow and led me over behind a pillar in the lobby.

"I am risking my job by telling you this," he said, glancing around cautiously, "but you are a very valued guest."

He glanced up at me expectantly.

"I really need this information," I said, looking at him steadily while slipping him another hundred dollar bill.

"Yes, sir," he said with muted glee. "Well, Mr. Askew, in fact, I watched a woman very much fitting the description you have given check out a little over an hour ago."

I threw my head back and let out a groan. The clerk scanned the lobby nervously.

"What was her name?" I whispered.

"Her name, sir?"

"Yes, her fucking name, what was it?" I hissed.

"Oh, Mr. Askew," he said, obviously disturbed by my manner. "I don't know. I didn't deal with her account."

"What?" I shouted. "How could you not know her name

when she's staying in your goddamned hotel?"

The lobby fell silent, the few people in it turning to observe us questioningly. As this was becoming the norm of all my social encounters, I did not pay the reaction any heed. But the clerk came alive, his eyes bulging, his forced smile nearly breaking his face.

"Oh, please, Mr. Askew," he said struggling to control his anxiety. "I am sure I can get you the information you need, if you will only give me some time."

"How long?"

"Just as quickly as possible, sir, I swear," said the clerk while smiling and nodding to various people staring at us.

"I assure you, Mr. Askew, if the information can be had, I will get it for you."

"I'm going up to my room now," I said in a calm, authoritative tone. "I'll be checking out in the next half an hour. Get my bill ready. Have a bellboy come up and get my luggage in fifteen minutes. Have my car brought around as well."

"And," I added in a low, threatening tone, "I'm counting on you to give me as much information about that woman as you can."

"Of course, Mr. Askew," replied the clerk, leaning back on his heals and fidgeting with his tie.

I went up to my room and packed like a man gone mad. Rushing here and there, I threw everything I could into an overpriced suit-bag I'd bought in the lobby and left the rest for the hotel staff. As I was hurrying out of my room, I met the clerk, who was near tears. My Darling had evidently anticipated pursuit by someone. She left special instructions that if her name were given out even by mistake to anyone, she would sue the Fairmont and the offending employee. This seemed incredible to me, but the clerk was so adamant and apparently near a nervous breakdown that I was sure it was true. Since he was my only link to her and my bullying had upset him so, I decided I must take a different tack.

I put my arm on his shoulder, which made him flinch. I told him he had done a fine job for me while giving him an additional hundred dollars. He managed a weary smile and thanked me with a sigh. I then assumed the air of a confidant, assuring him that no one would find out if he told me just a bit more about this woman. Could he not give me at least the direction she was headed?

"After all," I said in a soft, soothing tone while patting him on the back lightly, "it's not as though I'm out to hurt her. I just need to talk to her. That's all. It will be our little secret."

He appeared to struggle a bit more, but when I handed him my last hundred dollars, he finally caved in. He told me (at extreme risk to his job, he assured me yet again) the woman was returning to Los Angeles via Highway 1. How he knew this, he would not say. I pressed him for her name, but on that point, he would not relent. I decided not to waste more time trying to find out. After cashing a check for a thousand dollars, I gave the beleaguered clerk another hundred and then headed out.

I hadn't even gotten to the freeway, though, when I looked down and saw my gas gauge was on empty. I was frustrated beyond words, but I spent no emotion on the situation. I just pulled into a gas station, got out, and began to fill up the tank for my trek south.

"Hey man," I heard a voice say from behind me.

I looked up to a young black man in a bulky black San Francisco Giants jacket and baseball cap standing by the pump. I recognized the hungry look in his eyes; he was going to ask for money. The nine hundred dollars from the check I cashed was all wadded up in my pocket. I didn't like the idea of untangling it in front of anyone, especially this guy. His demeanor seemed aggressive, which made me wary.

"Man, you see that car over there," he said pointing to a late eighties yellow Ford Cougar. "That's my car, and I've been parked here for half the night, and these guys," he motioned to the gas station employees in the cashier's cubicle, "are gettin' tired a me hangin' around. Could I pull up behind you and get a little gas? Help me out, man. I wanna get outta here before they call the cops on me."

As he said all this, he looked from me to the Black Beauty back to me. He wore a sneering, cynical smile, like he knew I knew he was trying to pull one over on me and he didn't care.

"Sorry," I said while looking away. "I can't help you."

"Sure you can," he said curtly, smiling harshly and leaning forward slightly as though he was about to spring at me. "You could just give me a buck instead."

"I'm sorry," I said again.

"You're not sorry," he snapped.

I looked at him again. Hateful contempt had replaced the smile on his face

"Well," I said trying to keep my voice from wavering, "I can't help you."

"Yeah," he said making a slight step forward as he put his hand in his jacket. "Well, what *I* need is to get rich, and I *don't* need *you* to do it."

I flinched, thinking he was reaching for a gun. But he pulled out a wad of dollar bills instead and shook them at me. Then he shoved the money back in his pocket and walked away toward another patron pumping gas. I watched him stealthily as I went to pay. When I went back to my car, he ran over and got in the yellow Cougar. This made me nervous. I thought he could still have a gun even though he hadn't pulled one. Maybe he was coming to get me for refusing to "help" him. So when he pulled out behind me, a sick panic took hold of me.

I saw the freeway entrance just past a light two blocks ahead, so I gunned the Beauty to try and make the next light. The yellow Cougar stayed right on my tail as I did this, so I questioned my approach. Maybe I wouldn't lose him on the freeway. He might pull up next to me and shoot me dead. As I considered this, I unconsciously decreased my speed. A lane cleared next to me, and the Cougar darted into it. I was certain now that he was after me. My panic turned to pure fear, distracting me so that, only fifty yards from the intersection, I suddenly realized the light had turned red. I slammed on my brakes and went into a skid, screeching to a stop halfway in the crosswalk.

The Cougar stopped at the corner one lane over, apparently poised to make a quick getaway. The hustler jumped out of his car and smiled maniacally while glancing in my direction as he waited for the traffic to come to a halt. Early morning hour traffic was flowing through the intersection in front of me. I felt trapped, held like some sacrificial victim tied to an altar. The hustler started moving towards my car. I had to act or deal with a more menacing him. I smashed the accelerator to the floor. My tires squealing, I shot into the intersection. More tires squealed and horns blared. Had my window been down, I'm sure I would have caught a few of the expletives hurled after me as I careened up the ramp to the freeway.

With bloodshot eyes and white knuckles, near madness from fear and desire, I blazed down the freeway towards Highway 1. For the next half an hour, I was so shaken and frantic to leave the City behind that I could think of anything else. I kept checking my rearview mirror for the yellow Cougar but never saw it.

When I took the last exit to Highway 1, I finally began to relax. Phantasmagoric possibilities suddenly rose up and danced on the dim dawn horizon. I felt them leading me onward, pulling me forward into an unknown future now pregnant with potential, seeded with hope. Then, when I began to glide south down that world-renowned roadway, I felt the sublime surge of true belief reinstitute itself. And I liked it.

PART II
THE SEARCH CONTINUES

LOVE. All languages include this word. Though spellings or representations may vary, its meaning is always essentially the same. And although even that basic meaning can be articulated in many ways and with varying shades of subtlety, its ultimate meaning is manifested in one way: the feeling of completeness that only the *experience* of love can give to the soul.

Yet how often Love remains only a word, meaningless because of inaction. How many empty souls languish alone waiting for love to come to them, making no effort to find it because of fear or self-doubt? Driving south in pursuit of my Love, I looked out over the clear, blue waters of the Pacific and was stunned to recall that I had nearly become one of those lost souls. Of course, once I understood the situation, I had acted. But how had I been able to lead life before the knowledge of my particular Darling? How had only the general sense that someone was there been able to sustain me for so long? In light of this, I was amazed I hadn't thought of offing myself sooner.

I was also distraught at the idea that my Darling was still one of these wayward souls. Was she completely lost, I wondered? Would I be able to save her, or was she already too far gone to be redeemed? And what would constitute being too far gone? I thought of the Russian's experience. When he first told me his story, I'd been so overwhelmed to have my Love's existence confirmed I hadn't reflected on it. As I cruised through the misty seaside town of Half Moon Bay in those early morning hours, questions began to flood my brain. What state of mind must she have been in to do something like that? Was it an act calculated to corroborate the harsh cynicism she had adopted toward life, or was it a cry for help? Was she perhaps hoping that the Russian might turn out to be someone who could save her, someone capable of seeing through her jaded veneer and rescuing her from herself? But it must have been obvious to her after talking to him that he would be incapable of saving her, so why did she have sex with him? Could she have possibly hoped they might literally "make love?" What else could provoke her to commit such a random act?

She *must* have been hoping to "make love." How like me she was even in this act! She was not prepared to sit idly by waiting for me to come to her either. It was obvious to me that we were acting on similar impulses, already operating in synchronicity. And it even appeared that these impulses were grounded on the same philosophy: the pursuit of love. But she had found disappointment in the arms of the Russian; she very likely saw hers had been a desperate act.

For a few moments, I experienced feelings of tender solicitude for my Darling, but then another emotion began to muscle my compassion aside. It was an ugly reaction and a petty one, I admit, but I felt a smoldering jealousy burning inside me. Since she did not even know I existed, I knew how unfair this response was. But I couldn't help it. The thought of my Love in that clumsy oaf's arms caused me to cringe. In fact, I actually flinched so violently that I swerved into the oncoming traffic of the two-lane highway. A honking horn caused me to jerk the car wildly back to my lane. The horn honker, a little old lady with light purple hair in a powder blue '65 T-Bird, scowled and flipped me off as she went by.

After continuing down the road for a minute or so, I became confused about something. I noted particularly that it was a '65 T-bird. How had I known that? I could not really say. The jealousy I had been feeling about my Love's lack of fidelity was suddenly overwhelmed by a wave of melancholy. Then I remembered something I hadn't recalled for a very long time: my mother had had a '65 Thunderbird convertible. No sooner had I remembered this than a hazy memory of her and me driving down Highway 1 together surfaced in my consciousness. Another few moments reverie made me see the Oedipal ramifications of this recollection were, at very least, unpleasant to consider.

I had been resisting this connection to my quest since the Uncle Freddie episode when Cherice had fused my Darling's and my mother's stories together. But now it was too glaring to ignore. My estranged mother had died, and I was now following the same route she and I had once taken. But this time I felt I was in pursuit of the ultimate love of my life. What did it mean? Was all of what I was doing just a psychological script I was playing out in my life in order to deal with unresolved issues from my childhood? I knew that's what any therapist worth his salt (including many of those I had seen) would have concluded. This, of course, would have accounted for the (they would say) unsubstantiated drive I had toward my Darling, who I would have been perfectly willing to admit could have been interpreted simply as an Oedipal fantasy brought to life. So I was, once again and much to my chagrin, feeling confused and uncertain about everything I was doing. I decided to pull over at a rest stop and try to sort it out during a walk on the beach. I knew my Darling might be escaping me while I did this, but I had to resolve this conflict before I continued. The very validity of our love was at stake.

I turned into a driveway that led to a state-owned beach named San Gregario. Though the park gate was open, the large parking lot was completely empty. Tourists do not rise early in California, I supposed, due to the influence the state's lifestyle has on them. I parked and locked my car, then walked through a picnic area and down a flight of stairs to the beach. As I began walking south, I saw I had the whole place to myself, which I found a relief. The idea of someone idly fishing or absently combing the beach with a metal detector would have been annoying. I needed time alone to think and see a way through my apparently dream-deflating dilemma. For I could not continue to pursue my Darling if I were merely playing out some unconscious neurotic process. I needed a truly higher cause. I could not brook blind self-delusion, especially now that I had experienced what it felt like to be certain of my Darling's existence.

I began to think about my mother. My memories of her, especially of the trip we had taken down the coast, were hard to access at first. But after reflecting on it a bit, they came in a rush. The first and most prominent memory was of the time we spent at the Boardwalk amusement park in Santa Cruz. We played games for prizes and rode the miniature train five times. I remember crying because I wanted to go on the roller coaster, but I was too small. I cried so hard that eventually my mother started crying too. When I saw this, I quit crying and began to try to console her. But this only seemed to make her cry harder, so I just stood there and waited for her to stop.

After that, I had a hot dog. My mother watched me with moist eyes and smiled at me while I ate. She had nice white teeth and a pretty oval face. Her hair was sandy blonde, and she wore it straight and long, just past her shoulders. I recalled a comfort from her smile, which — I realized as I reflected back on it — I had never really known since.

The next thing I remembered was driving down the coast with the top down in the T-bird. I could not see above the door without stretching and straining my neck, and so most of the views from the highway were blocked to me. I spent much of the time looking at my mother as a result. Watching her had given me the feeling she and I were on some sort of a quest. I recalled that, though she had been kind to me, she seemed distracted by something. I remembered specifically a time when she was standing in front of me on a small hill near a turnout we'd pulled into which overlooked the ocean. She had her hand up to shelter her eyes from the setting sun, which made her only a silhouette to me. As she stood there, I remembered thinking her a rescuer of some sort, scouring the horizon for something or someone who was lost. This was the image I saw clearly as I walked along the beach. Still, at the time, I could not reckon with why she seemed sad to me.

But then I began to consider her in the light of what I knew happened after this trip, and things began to make sense. I had the feeling I was around four, which meant she would have left my father soon thereafter. When I realized this, I understood, at least in part, why she was distracted and sad. Obviously, she was wrestling with whether or not to leave my father and me.

I stopped in my tracks at this last thought.

And *me*. I could hardly believe it myself, but I can honestly say that for the first time in my life, it became real to me that my mother had left me when I was only a child. Only one thought went through my mind: How could she have done it? How could a mother leave her child? What circumstance could have justifiably led to such a breach of maternal duty, that primitive impulse that can lead women to risk life and limb in order to save their offspring?

As I turned and began to walk back to my car, I tried to

consider the potential reasons for this irreconcilably unnatural act. Perhaps my father had beat or harmed her in some way. I had no memories of this. But I had next to no memories of any home life with my mother either, so it was not implausible. In all the time I had known him, though, my father had never been a violent person. Maybe it was the residue of his peace activism in the Sixties. With my step-mother and half-brother, he was as gentle as a koala bear. Besides, though I couldn't have said just how, I knew my mother would never have left me with him if she knew he was violent.

Perhaps she was afraid she would not be able to support the two of us on her own. I could empathize with this fear. Even with a college education, a woman in those days might still have felt daunted by the prospect of single parenthood. But surely my father would have helped her. Whatever the rift between them may have been, he would have invariably been compelled to help her as a result of his intense sense of duty and responsibility. My grandparents would also have seen to this even if he hadn't. They may have seemed rigid and unapproachable, but I recall that when they did speak of her, which was rarely, they always used words of affection. Given their austere demeanor, this spoke heavily in favor of the above theory.

After considering these two alternatives, I decided there was probably no way I could ever truly know why my mother had left me with my father, no matter how many theories I considered. I knew asking my father why she had done it would be useless as well because I sensed that even he didn't know. Who can ever truly know what motivates a human being to do one thing or another? But I did wonder where this unresolved conclusion left me. Again, any psychologist worth a damn would have put my quest for my Love down to the pursuit of the love I did not receive from my estranged mother; and I knew it would have been a difficult theory to rationally refute. Still, I could not help but resist any characterization which equated the love I felt for my Darling with some Pavlovian dog-like reaction to a childhood trauma. Surely all the things about my Darling and our love in which I had found so much hope and redemption could not be explained away so simply as that!

By this time, I had reached the stairs that led back to the parking lot from the beach. I walked up the stairs and stood in the picnic area staring over at my Black Beauty, which seemed to whinny and stamp its feet in anticipation of heading back to the road. I could not, however, proceed in pursuit of my Love without coming to some sort of resolution. I wandered over to a monument situated in the middle of the greenbelt area parallel to the parking lot. I sat down on the two-foot high railing, which was meant somehow to protect the monument, and read the plaque mounted on the cement obelisk.

It seems I was sitting in the former Portolà Camp, which was struck by Captain Gaspar de Portolà "and his party of Spanish explorers" in 1769. According to the plaque — placed there by the Centennials Commission, whoever they were — Portolà and his chums had set out over land to find Monterey Bay, but their effort was "fruitless." They had then stopped where I sat at San Gregario Creek for three days in October to rest and nurse their sick. I paused to take a look around. Though the vast blue rolling ocean being fed by the meandering creek and the green vegetation which clung close to the surrounding hills were beautiful, I imagined that the Captain and his party might not have been as apt to appreciate that beauty in the circumstance they were in. Lost and nursing their sick in a completely foreign land, I figured there might possibly have been a morale problem in the Portolà Camp. Whispers of quitting and heading back to civilization must have passed on the lips of his men. The sick must have asked themselves why they did it. What had they been thinking of when they left their safe and comfortable homes in Spain? Had the potential for glory truly been worth such a risk of their lives? In thinking of these things, I found myself feeling a sense of solidarity with Portolà and his men. I, too, had started out in search of something great and now, like them, felt lost and sick and wondered what it was I was doing out in this wide world alone on an apparently mad pursuit.

But I had not read the last line about the Portolà party. Evidently, all had not been failure for the good Captain and his compatriots, as the plaque went on to flat-footedly note: "Having missed Monterey, they later discovered San Francisco Bay instead."

I chuckled over this phrasing, which was so quintessentially American. No flowery embellishments, just the straightforward facts, ma'am. Of course, cynic that I was, I assumed this matter-of-fact phrasing was also due to the fact that it had been the Spanish and not some Anglo explorer who'd made this enormous discovery. The plaque was put there in nineteen forty-nine, so this would have fit the current political climate. Fresh from the success of WWII and pre-Korea, who would have wanted to even slightly sully the glory of America by giving credit to some lucky foreigners ? But perhaps I was being too harsh. Maybe the thought hadn't even crossed the minds of the members of the Centennials Commission.

I got up and started to walk to my car. As I did this, I looked around again at the lovely scenery and thought of Portolà himself. I wondered if he might also have entertained thoughts of uncertainty such as I attributed to his men. But even if he had, he did go on to discover San Francisco Bay, which was a much greater accomplishment than he had set out to do. And then it suddenly struck me: I might be like Portolà in this respect as well. Even if my sub-conscious had been leading me by the nose in some attempt to fulfill an Oedipal fantasy, what was to keep me from transcending that goal and achieving an even greater one ? Not a thing, I thought. Absolutely nothing! I let out a yelp of joy and leaped in the air, then started to run over toward my car.

More people had arrived for a day at the beach, and a park employee was now taking money from those lined up down the driveway. Only the park employee taking money in a kiosk at the entrance looked over at me when I yelped. When I started running toward my car he beckoned me over. As I got closer to him I saw that "he" was actually a "she" who happened to be rather large. My mistake was a simple one to have made for more reasons than her size, though. She was dressed in a gender dissembling state-issued park uniform: a pair of dark drab green pants, a dull olive green shirt, a dark brown baseball cap with the state park emblem — a round patch with golden background and a brown Grizzly in profile — plus a pair of heavy boots. The culminating result was a being whose sex was definitely difficult to discern from a distance. Her breasts, which I was able to distinguish from her mass of flesh only when close by, were the only way I was able to be certain of her sex.

"Is that your black car over there?" she asked.

"Yes, it is, my dear," I said playfully.

I was in a good mood now that my purpose was once again secure.

A smile played across her chubby face, and her eyes seemed to brighten a bit, betraying her youth. She couldn't have been more than twenty or so. Her face then puckered up into an apologetic expression, and she said:

"Well, I'm sorry, but I have to get three dollars from you."

"Absolutely, positively, no problem, my good young lady," I said, while handing her a twenty. "And you seem so very pleasant that I insist on you keeping the change."

"Oh," she said breathily, her mustached upper lip quivering slightly as she looked about apprehensively. "I can't do that. It's against park policy."

Moving closer to her, I looked around with mock cunning,

then said, "We'll just keep it between ourselves. It'll be our little secret."

A rusting silver late '70s model Chevy had pulled up next to us and the driver, an unshaven, motley-looking white male, distracted her by holding out his three dollars. I walked quickly over to my car. As I drove past her little bungalow on the way out, she waved and beamed a big smile. I waved back to her airily and turned happily onto the highway and back on the trail of my Darling.

∼

SINCE I'D WASTED SO MUCH TIME during my beach musings, I decided to make double time getting to Santa Cruz. Shooting down the highway at a blinding speed, what I'm sure is a beautiful landscape was but a blur.

When I approached Santa Cruz, I began to slow down. I did this not only because of my concern about getting a speeding ticket but also because I wanted to consider whether or not to stop. The speed had helped burn some of the pent-up energy I had after San Gregario. And when I caught a glimpse of the serene Monterey Bay, I grew almost tranquil. As a result, my attitude toward Santa Cruz as I approached it was one of benevolence. Tooling down the apparent main drag, Mission Blvd., I found a lack of many things (strip malls and the like) I was sure my Dearest would find equally loathsome. I thought, Yes, maybe I'll find her here.

But just then, as I unsuspectingly rounded a gradual turn, *it* appeared before me. On the white brick wall of a burned-out building, scrawled in large, black, spray-painted letters, stood a message to all literate passers-by:

LESBIANISM: NOT JUST THE FUNNEST THING YOU COULD THINK OF, BUT A FORCE.

I was not shocked by this sign, but it did heighten both my curiosity and awareness. The people I'd seen up to this point had seemed harmless enough. For the most part, they wore tye-dye or loose-fitting clothes and appeared to be either laid-back beach folks or hippies. So after I saw this declaration, I began to look in the cars on the road with me, trying not to let this "force," or rather the force the sign had created in my mind, distort how I saw them. But either I didn't succeed or there was some sort of militant feminist rally taking place close by to which almost every woman I saw was headed. Nearly every woman I looked at for longer than a few seconds glared back as though she wished I did not exist.

Now of the two forms of homosexuality of which I'm aware, I find the idea of women turning to other women the most understandable. Given their options (celibacy, bestiality, or involvement with men on any level), I am often surprised they don't choose it more often. And I knew my Love would have disdain for men in general since they were ruling members of contemptible humanity. Obviously — as my search for my

Darling betrayed — I could not believe she was compelled by nature to pursue that lifestyle exclusively. That she may have experimented, I could accept. But that she had remained in that camp, I could not. So I was certain she would not choose the company of those who did, at least not to the degree displayed in Santa Cruz.

Still, I was driven somehow to go into the city. Something about that open hostility toward my mere being was attractive to me. Maybe it was my recollection of the blonde in San Francisco. Maybe I couldn't resist the desire to make myself more than just my gender to one of these women. I couldn't help thinking of the purple-haired girl as well. For some reason, I regretted that she had detested me so. Even though the thought of her actually intimidated me to that moment, I still wished I could have made her like me, if only a little. So, instead of turning left at the light off Mission back to Highway 1, I continued forward on to Santa Cruz.

The road curved and went down a hill to another stoplight where an old brick clock tower sat with dignity to the left of the intersection. But down the street to the right looked like a war zone. The shattered landscape, I felt safe in assuming, was the result of the '89 earthquake. Interspersed between the buildings, some of them barely standing, I could see enormous holes. People were on the streets moving amidst the rubble; it was a clear day and the sun was shining. And yet, I felt a heaviness of spirit about the place. Well over two years had passed, but I would have believed the quake had been only a week before.

The eeriness I've heard accompanies all mass tragedies still clung to the air there in Santa Cruz. I continued forward in spite of the foreboding look of the place.

Signs with directions to the Boardwalk had been confronting me as I entered the town, which sparked the memory of my musings on the beach. When I saw yet another, I got an idea. Why not go and ride the roller coaster at the amusement park? That would surely help bury once and for all those memories, as well any potency they might still have. Then I could move on toward my Darling unhindered by any potential Oedipal implications of my quest.

I was at the Boardwalk in a matter of minutes. The sight of that huge roller coaster and the screams of its riders vividly brought to mind the time my mother and I shared there. As I walked to the entrance, I did feel some apprehension. But the longing I felt to dive to the pit of my psychological uncertainty and lay waste to whatever might lurk there waiting to sabotage my dream was stronger. I went straight to the ticket booth and purchased enough tickets to ride that machine fifty times if I found it necessary.

As I passed the various games of chance, the barkers tried to entice me to their booths with subtle challenges to my manhood. I was unfazed. But I had had nothing to eat all day, and my stomach was becoming upset, so I did make one quick stop to devour four hot dogs and an enormous Pepsi. I then made my way through the riffraff swarming the promenade straight to The Big Dipper (as the roller coaster was named). To my relief, the line was short, and I was forced to wait only a few minutes.

When I was admitted, I fought my way past the screaming children up to the first car, which I jumped in and pulled the restraining bar down to keep anyone from joining me. A lanky, prepubescent boy began to make a stink over wanting to sit in front with me. But I would not budge. I was intent on confronting my demons alone. In a matter of seconds, a pimply-faced teenage boy dressed in the stiff, hideous orange and brown polyester Boardwalk uniform was on me. He told me with unmasked hostility that I would have to share the car with another person or not ride at all. Digging down in my pocket, I came up with a hundred dollar bill. I asked him to lean down by me, which he did with hesitation. I slid the bill along with the rest of my tickets into his unsuspectingly open hand. I then requested that he tell the lanky little shit that I owned the park and could ride by myself in the front car as long as I wanted. Nearly bounding with joy at his serendipity, Pimple Face ushered the lanky boy to the back car, then started the ride.

The first five times around were unremarkable. The rushing and hurtling of the rackety car on the rickety track did not affect me. I tried to feel as though I were being heroic about this, like I was withstanding the slings and arrows of an advancing enemy with brave indifference. But since I had not experienced the sense of closure I had been expecting, I felt I was not truly facing up to my demons. Just exactly what it was I was hoping to feel I could not have said. I knew, however, that I hadn't felt it yet. On top of all this, the next time around, I began to feel a bit queasy.

Although I have not mentioned it, The Big Dipper was appropriately named. And after my eighth time around, my green face would have silently, but effectively, borne witness to this. I was not the only one observing my physical state. My recent beneficiary, Pimple Face, began to watch me nervously each time I came round. He was growing concerned that the lanky kid would rat on him, no doubt. So between the uneasy looks he was giving me, my anxiety about not feeling whatever it was I was hoping to feel, and my stomach's advancing upheaval, I felt like one of those ripe, ready to burst zits on Pimple Face. But I was sure the next time around would be the decisive trip. And indeed it was.

We lurched out of the Big Dipper's bay to the foot of the initial hill. The mechanism that pulls the cars up the incline attached itself, then began to chuggingly draw us upward. We reached the top, and, as on all roller coasters, there was a momentary pause. The view was lovely: the bay, the beach, the cute little cottages on the hills surrounding the park. I rather enjoyed that moment; almost forgot where I was. This was probably the reason the rush of the first drop caught me so off guard, causing me to vomit at least half of the contents of my stomach in that one fell swoop. And as I had turned to take in the view, my head was jerked back simultaneously, sending all that came up directly behind me.

The screams I had grown used to hearing behind me took

on a decidedly different quality. Squeals that once conveyed the thrilling release of pent-up anticipation and excitement turned to shrieks of genuine horror and disgust. I was only able to note this change in passing, however, because we were nearing our next precipitous descent, and I felt another heave coming on. I leaned out from the cars to try and keep from spraying my fellow riders another time. This, however, had unfortunate results. Because of the thrust from the drop, my head was again thrown backward and my "line of fire," if you will, was much more direct. The passengers in the car immediately behind me (two very attractive girls in their late teens) got the worst of it. But those in back of them were not spared completely. This last retch evidently finished off the contents of my stomach, because, though I continued to slump over the side of my car and feel dreadful, nothing else came up. In spite of this good fortune, nearly everyone cried and moaned for the remainder of the ride.

The scene on the disembarkation platform approached pandemonium; like triage on M.A.S.H., people laid out here and there receiving help according to their need. Having heard the screams and assessed the situation, Pimple Face was now rushing to and fro with a roll of paper towels and a look of sheer horror on his scarred face. I rested for a moment, ignobly ducking forward out of sight in hopes of an opportunity to quietly slip away. When Pimple Face went to find another roll of towels, I saw my chance. Leaping to the platform, I raced for the exit. But my quick movement caught the attention of a mother attending her quivering, vomit-laden child.

"It was him!" she screamed in a shrill voice. "He was the one that did it!"

I felt all eyes and energy on the platform turn on me. But I did not break my stride. Suddenly, in the exit in front of me, Pimple Face appeared with an armful of rolls of paper towels. His eyes went wide with fear and loathing as I dashed straight at him. He let out a groan when I body-blocked him to the ground. Rolls of paper towels flew up and out like frightened birds. I heard a great clamor behind me as I ran through the exit, but I did not stop running. When I got to the Black Beauty, I jumped in and spun out of the parking lot and off to the highway.

~

BACK ON HIGHWAY 1, I felt not as if I were driving, but soaring: through the mountains and pines, over the rolling farmland and sand dunes toward Monterey. The air was crisp, the sky was azure, and my Darling was waiting for me only just down the road, I was sure. If doubts came again, Faith, born from my time at San Gregario and in Santa Cruz, would eschew them. Everyone and everything I encountered I would now view not as obstacles but rather as facilitators — the means to my Love. I knew this would be difficult for me, even a test. But I felt worthy and capable of enduring that now. I had faced my deepest fears and come out the winner. What could life throw at me that I could not deal with?

The Monterey area seemed open and inviting when I finally reached it after around forty minutes. I decided it would be best to stop, get a room, and clean myself up a bit. Besides, the rugged coast with its gnarled cypress trees, jagged rocks, and pounding surf inspired me. I knew my Darling must have stopped to drink all this in as well. Then, as I approached the first exit to Monterey, I had a vision of my Love strolling on the beach at night. The moon, obscured now and again by wisps of clouds in a late-night sky, cast its lustrous light upon her. I felt certain the terrain was Carmel, but I was not close enough to distinguish my Darling's features, of course. The image burst like a bubble when a delivery truck cut me off as it merged onto the highway. Now I knew I had to stop, if for nothing else but to walk the beach at least one night to try to fulfill this vision.

Cars were backed for a mile up the highway trying to squeeze their way down into Carmel via small surface streets ill designed for the traffic. Because of the sun, my clothes were growing sour, but my spirits did not waver. I remained upbeat, thinking of how I could laughingly recall all of this to my Sweet; she would, of course, playfully mock me, but would admire me for my tenacity.

The line of cars inched its way toward the ocean, and soon I was in the middle of Carmel. The streets were alive with tourists who milled up and down the shop-lined avenues. As in San Francisco, they all seem in an inexplicably ecstatic state, almost awed. That the narrow streets with over-hanging trees lent a certain charm to the place, I could not deny. But the throngs of people and unrelenting sales pitch of the "quaint little shops" sapped it of whatever potential allure it might have possessed.

As they gawked at me and my Black Beauty, I felt a pity for these people rather than antipathy, as I would have before my purge. Pretty though it was, the idea that a place so glutted with their fellow man could be such an enormous source of pleasure to them made them very sad to me. Was this the representative high-point of a vacation some of them may have been saving for all their lives? What kind of life could they have if such an experience could be enjoyable to them? I knew my Darling must have felt the same as me and wondered if she would have stayed despite her reaction. In the end, I decided she, like myself, would probably have needed a brief rest as well. Just an overnight stay to bolster her for the drive ahead. There was also my vision, which I could not ignore even for the sake of expediency. I drove down several blocks after reaching the city square before finding a place in front of an art gallery to park. I went into the gallery in hopes of finding a local to suggest an appropriately up-scale place to stay.

In the back of the showroom, a well-tanned, urban-looking man sat behind a small, modern black desk wearing black pants, a black turtle-neck, and an off-white cardigan sweater. In spite of his silver hair and thin, reptilian lips, he appeared relatively young, possibly around my father's age. He had remained seated as I came in, displaying straight, white teeth as he smiled what was an oddly cold yet inviting smile while bowing his head slightly. I smiled, glanced around, then walked over to a hideous sculpture of stereotypical jazz musicians melded together and writhing apparently in an attempt to escape from the shared humiliation of their pose. The price tag hung conspicuously from an upwardly-pointed clarinet: a mere twenty-five hundred dollars.

"That's a wonderful piece, don't you think?" the man stated nonchalantly.

"Yes, wonderful," I remarked. "I don't suppose you'd sell it to me, would you?"

Before you could say "substantial commission," he was at my elbow. But when he reached olfactory range, a slight yet detectable wince passed over his face. As I positively reeked by this point, I was impressed with how well he was able to conceal his nausea. He crowned his success by smiling and saying almost liltingly:

"Of course, we would be only too happy to sell you whatever you'd like."

"Well, then I'll take this sculpture, and I think I like that painting," I said, pointing to an enormous, ghastly watercolor of a steeplechase. "It's not too much, is it?"

"Only fifteen hundred dollars, sir!" he said, taking the opportunity to move away from me by gliding over and making a sweeping gesture from the bottom to the top of the painting as though he were a show-model on "The Price is Right."

"Perfect!" I chirped. "Now, let's see…"

I then picked out eight more high priced, aesthetically impoverished pieces. Of course, I took every chance to get near the salesman, who in turn took every legitimate opportunity to put distance between us. Once, however, I forced him to stand next to me for several minutes while I questioned him in detail regarding the artist's brushwork in an oil painting of a local seascape. By posing questions that required longer responses, I was sure he was forced to breathe through his nose at least a few times. I even went so far as to put my arm on his shoulder, pulling him closer to me under the pretense of pointing out some non-existent detail in some atrocious pencil sketch I eventually bought.

I soon grew tired of torturing the poor man, though, so I gave him my American Express card to pay for the tripe I'd picked out. While he was calling in for approval of the sizable purchase, I asked if there was an exclusive hotel near a beach in which I might stay. With the strange, reserved, casual enthusiasm all who serve the rich deploy, he recommended an inn just down the street which had ocean views and was only a few blocks from Carmel Beach.

Everything was just fine with me until he began to write down the approval number for the fifteen plus thousand dollars I'd pissed off. I noted a strange reaction in myself. A physical sense of revulsion took hold of me. So much so that, combined with the stench of my clothes, I felt the urge to convulse again as I had on The Big Dipper. As I signed for my purchases, I was truly afraid I was going to vomit all over the salesman's desk. So when he snatched his pen from my hand and began to prepare a final receipt, I jumped up and ran from the gallery. Once outside in the cool air, I felt a little better. But I was still a touch nauseous, so I left my car and trotted toward the ocean at a brisk pace.

The sidewalks were crowded, so I dashed through the parked cars and started running along the side of the road. I garnered stares as I ran, but I didn't care. I only felt good while running. The moist air under the low-branched trees refreshed me as I jogged along, but after several blocks, my stomach was still uneasy. When I reached the street the inn the salesman recommended was on, I decided to risk stopping. To keep my head from swimming, I bent down and put it between my knees. From my upside-down view, I could see the tourists ogling, but that was the only position in which I didn't feel sick, so I stuck to it. After a minute or so, I was able to raise my head and walked back to my car. The thought of dealing with the salesman did not appeal to me, so I just got in my Beauty and drove to the inn. I checked in and began to clean my foul-smelling self up.

I was enjoying a long hot shower when I heard the phone ring. I left the shower running and answered it. It was the salesman. He had tracked me down to ask in a wary, perplexed voice where I wanted the pieces I'd purchased to be delivered. Without a thought, I told him to donate them to a local charity and hung up. I felt a sudden sense of relief. I recalled I'd had nearly the same reaction when giving money to the homeless in San Francisco. I wondered what was going on with me that I seemed to be repeating this behavior.

But I pondered it only a moment. I was tired of trying to

figure myself out. I had already gone through so much of that. I decided it would be better from this point forward just to let my impulses take me where they might. Having wrestled with my most major concern (my possible Oedipal motivations) and come out with a satisfactory resolution, I saw no need to make an issue out of every odd thing I did. I realized — shrewdly I think — that, if I wasn't careful, I could waste all my time in self-absorbed reflection rather than in pursuit of my Darling. After all, it was she, not me, who was in jeopardy. So I let it go and dressed for a quiet dinner.

Before leaving, I checked myself out in the mirror. I saw a perfect picture of function melded with fashion. My elegant black Canali suit, stunning with its subtle gray pinstripes, would force any woman of taste (such as my Love) to take note. And my black high-top Converse tennies, laced up and tied at the top to keep the sand out in anticipation of my beach stroll. All indicated a man not of the plebeian ilk, incapable of planning for expected eventualities, but rather a man with admirable foresight; a man with whom any woman would be proud, even grateful, to share a profound love.

～

UNFORTUNATELY, dinner did not turn out to be the pleasant prelude to finding my Love I had planned. Not knowing any place to dine, I asked the innkeeper where to go. He suggested a petite French bistro named (with the cultural incongruity typical of pretentious Americans) Casanova's. Though it was very nearly too precious with its quaint little French Country motif, it was not the restaurant that bothered me. In fact, the food was delicious, and the service was more than adequate. The waiter was unobtrusively present, promptly delivering aperitifs, appetizers, entree, wine, and after dinner drinks.

What bothered me was the couple seated next to me during the last half of my meal. They appeared to be inoffensive enough when they first sat down. He had a slightly pudgy face and a jaw that threatened to recede into his neck in diminishing old age. His looks were redeemed by tousled dark hair and blue eyes with thick lashes, which gave him an innocent little-boy look. She had a round face, except for her chin, which jutted out to a narrow point, green eyes, and short-cropped blonde hair. On her small frame were clothes which matched - and were obviously calculated to do so - with pathetic perfection.

It wasn't even their appearance that annoyed me, though. It was their saccharine way of carrying on with one another. Oh, they tried to be subtle about it. They didn't let too much show. Only a "sugar" here or a "honeybun" there. But after watching them a while, I was sure that when they were out of the public eye they did actually coo and cluck in the most sickening way. Another person might not have drawn this conclusion, but I was a cunning observer. I saw through their façade. That they were restraining themselves made it nauseating to watch because it was obvious they were conscious that what they were doing was pathetic. Yet they did it anyway. In fact, they seemed to enjoy it for that very reason. This self-conscious, self-mocking seemed to me a mortal sin. It ran contrary to why I was pursuing my Darling.

Their behavior put me in a morose mood. I ordered another cognac to counteract my response , but it did not help. I found myself scowling because of them. I kept these scowls to myself initially. Soon, however, I could not resist shooting venomous glances in their direction. At first, they were too self-absorbed to notice. By the time I was on my third drink, though, they had both observed me openly glaring at them. Her reaction was to grow nervous and throw fretful looks in my direction, then back to her mate. He tried smiling at me to defuse the situation, going so far as to say, "Hello," once. But when I continued my antagonistic posture, he became agitated, then finally got angry.

"Hey, what's your problem, man!?" he growled harshly, his face red with anger.

"My problem," I replied without hesitation, "is that you and your fucking wife make me want to puke the lovely meal I just had all over this table in front of me."

Her mouth dropped open, and his eyes bulged in outraged disbelief. He was preparing to leap to his feet when the manager, who happened to be walking by, interceded.

"Sir," he declared brusquely. "I am going to have to ask you to pay your bill and leave. We cannot accept such behavior."

"Oh yeah," I screamed as I stood to my feet, knocking my chair to the ground, "so I can't speak my mind when it's me who's been wronged by them, huh? Well, just because it's your policy to let people like those two sit over there and ruin my meal with their offensive behavior doesn't mean I have to take it!"

I threw several hundred dollar bills on the table and marched out through the once boisterous, now completely silent restaurant. Once outside, I calmed down immediately. I was elated by the fortuitous timing of this little episode. The moon and the stars were casting a light almost exactly like that in my vision. The hour was upon me, and I had to get to the beach as quickly as possible. Fortunately, I had already asked the innkeeper the directions, so I simply headed off to fulfill my destiny.

∼

AFTER ONLY A TEN MINUTE WALK down the narrow, unlit residential streets, I reached Carmel Beach. But looking out over it, I saw it was all wrong. It looked nothing like the beach in my vision. This was extremely disheartening, because everything else was just right. The light from the moon, the pounding surf, the iridescent glow of the sand: all perfect, except for the beach itself, which was too narrow and did not afford a view of hills as in my vision. Not willing to accept this as a defeat, I began to wonder if maybe there wasn't another beach further down the road. I stood there a moment considering whether I should risk missing my Dear on this beach while searching for a nonexistent other. But studying it a few moments longer, I made up my mind that I must risk it. I had to follow my vision to the last detail, using it like a map to my Love.

I began to walk south along the shore. The road turned to the right and the beach abruptly ended. The shore then consisted of a ten-foot cliff at the foot of which lay twisted, jagged volcanic rock. The ocean crashed and foamed against these black masses. Waves broke, then came an eerie whispery sucking sound, then the waves broke violently again. My way was now well-lit by the moon, which had been obscured before by a thick overhang of trees. The houses along the narrow road remained dark, though, and seemed to shun me, pushing me against the unfriendly shore. Looking out to a dark pine-covered point across the bay, I followed the shoreline back to me. I was sure I saw a beach across the water, but I was also sure it would take at least an hour to get there. The light from the moon was beginning to approach the hue it had been in my vision, and I began to fear I wouldn't reach the predesignated spot in time. I considered scaling the rocks and diving into the ocean but decided I had had too much to drink and doubled my pace to a quick jog instead.

The light was changing with each passing moment, and I grew more and more frantic that I might not meet my Darling at the preordained time. Spurred by this fear, I abandoned my trot and broke into a run. The road had been narrowing and I was afraid it might deadend at any moment, forcing me to resort to my earlier plan of swimming across the bay. I shivered at the thought of the cold water. But then I pictured myself rising from the surf and striding up to my Love like Burt Lancaster in *From*

Here to Eternity, the sheer romance of which made me seriously consider it, whether it proved necessary or not. After all, my Darling would hardly be able to resist such a vigorous display of masculinity.

The beach still looked miles away, and I was preparing to descend to the water when I rounded a corner and beheld a vast expanse of sand. I stopped in place, awestruck by what I saw. The beach of my vision, as though it had been poured directly from my mind into reality, lay before me. Under a cypress tree I could see a railing. I rushed down the steps and out onto the sand.

The moon's milky light covered the white sand and the treetops and the yellow grass on the high, rolling hills behind Carmel. Everything glowed preternaturally. The air was heavy with moisture from the pounding surf, which was throwing white spray into the moonlight. In all I sensed the untapped potential of the moment. It weighed in on me, importuning me in some way to act. I felt inspired. I walked down the beach, drinking it all in. I wanted to call out to my Love, to summon her like a muse.

After only a few minutes of walking, however, it was me who felt a call: the familiar twinge of my too-full bladder. All the wine and after dinner drinks I'd had apparently decided *en masse* that they had spent enough time in my body. Though irritated by this prosaic interruption, I was not too upset because circumstances did not require me to resist the call. I scurried over behind an ice-plant covered dune and unsheathed myself.

This was not an all-consuming occupation, so I kept my head just above the top of the dune to maintain a line of sight and surveyed the beach.

As I was finishing up, I saw her. A well-formed young woman with long dark hair stood out in the full light of the moon a few hundred yards away near the stairs. I had not seen her come onto the sand ; it was as though she had just appeared. And I realized as I looked on that the scene was the physical embodiment of my vision.

I was struck dumb. I could not move. My mouth gaped open, and my arms hung heavy at my sides. Only my eyes were left to observe. With them, I saw my Love (for I was convinced it was her) as she stood for several minutes looking out at the ocean. Then suddenly, she dropped to her knees and raised her arms to the clear night sky. The breath felt as if it had been sucked from my lungs. In this grand gesture, I saw an act raw in its desperation. This was a plea to an eternal being, I was sure, a plea to be saved from something profound, something oppressive and awesome. I was moved to the depths of my soul. Before I could think, a plaintive cry came to my lips:

"Love, I am here!"

My Darling leaped to her feet and stood scanning in the direction of where I stood behind the sand dune. Each and every fiber of my being screamed for me to run to her, but for some inexplicable reason, I still could not move. Even from the distance we were at, I could see that she, too, was frozen in place.

"Darling, your prayers are answered," I managed to cry

out. "It's me, your one true love. I've come to save you!"

As I said this I was, to my utter joy, able to break free from whatever had been holding me. I took a step forward, then another, then another, until at last I began to run. True, it was more stumbling than running, but I was at least making measurable progress. My excitement at this progress, however, quickly dissipated when I saw the goal I was moving toward bounding like a frightened gazelle toward the steps.

"Darling, stop!" I shouted. "Love, it is I! Stop and wait for your salvation to reach you!"

I thought this would surely make her see her mistake. It seemed instead to light a fire under her. She only glanced over her shoulder then sprinted even faster than before, appearing to almost glide across the sand. In spite of the fact that her desire to elude me was the reason for this display, I felt a sincere pleasure in observing how lithe her movements were. Through this unexpected exhibition of physical grace and beauty, my Dearest appeared like some wingless angel come to favor we mortals with a show of her heavenly talents. As she neared the stairs, my heart was nearly bursting with pride. What a prize I had in her!

At that moment, I surged forward and tumbled head over heels into a somersault, then landed face first in the sand. I tossed my head up immediately, spat out a mouthful of sand and shook myself violently like a Labrador retriever fresh from the water. When I regained my feet, I saw what had caused this tumble. In my haste to reach my Dearest, I had neglected to zip up and button my pants. I had gone around twenty-five yards before they snared me at my ankles. When I pulled them back to my waist, my head came up in time to see my Dearest disappear into the shade by the stairs.

"Love!" I screamed . "Love, wait for me!"

I ran toward the stairs as fast as I could, which was none too swift since I was in sand and was forced to hold my pants up as well. I scanned the light at the top of the stairs and saw my Love enter it then dart back into the black shadows of one of the residential streets. I was so winded that I was barely able to make it to the last step by the time I reached the stairs. Running with a stomach full of petite filet, sautéed vegetables, and baked potato, not to mention two bottles of Bordeaux and many before and after dinner drinks had made me sick. Still, I knew I must continue after her. After taking a moment to zip up and secure my pants, I headed off into the shadows at the only pace I could maintain by that point: a steady lope.

∼

I HAD STOPPED CRYING OUT FOR HER. I didn't want to draw attention to myself on the quiet street. Aside from this, I had just seen her ignore my cries, so I knew I had to abandon that approach. As I pressed forward, however, it concerned me that she had ignored my pleas. She must have heard me. Could she really have not recognized me? Or was she just toying with me to prolong the agony of my separation from her? But she must be in agony too, so why would she run from relief if it was so near? I could hardly believe emotional masochism would be her style. In the end, I decided she must not have recognized me, though this was a hard conclusion to swallow on such a full stomach.

I scanned each house I passed for any lights. Because of the late hour, nearly all were dark. Even those with lights on looked uninviting and impregnable. I had been jogging along like this for quite a while and was approaching Ocean Blvd., the main drag, when I heard voices just ahead. Irritated at the thought of interacting with, let alone acknowledging, anyone but my Darling, I leaped into some bushes next to the road to wait for them to pass.

As they approached, I could see they were lovers from the way their shadowy figures clung to one another, which made my situation doubly bitter. The woman — a short, waddling butterball — was snuggling into the man's mountainous body while he draped an Orangutan-like arm over her shoulder. They were an odd-looking couple, but something about them began to look familiar as they drew near. I was struggling to place them when they stopped abruptly, only a few feet away. Even though my eyes had grown somewhat adjusted to the darkness, the trees obscured the moon and stars, preventing me from making out their faces. But I did not need my eyes, nor would I have wanted them, after the man in a husky whisper uttered these ghastly, all too illuminating words:

"Charlotte, you could run a flag straight up my pole right now. Let's do it in the bushes like we did that time in Tulsa."

I was paralyzed. I could not have imagined two people I would have wanted to see engaged in any type of amorous sport less than that fat, blithering pair. Charlotte began to giggle, and I prayed with the fervor of a man in deep peril that some moralistic fiber in her being would awake and revolt against this licentious suggestion. But, to my horror, she offered only a few token words of resistance concerning the discomfort and the cold, then yielded and cooed:

"Oh, my little romantic Neddy Bear!"

I felt like an animal in a trap. I wanted to leap up and run, but something held me irresistibly to my place. The two of them plopped down only a foot or so from where I huddled in place and began groping and grabbing at each other with the zeal of hormonally charged teenagers. With their every subdued gasp and moan of pleasure, I responded in kind with internal gasps and moans of abomination. Each second seemed years, every minute an eternity. I hunkered down in the bushes with the stillness of a hunted fawn and prayed for the end to come. But their passion for one another and this reckless adventure seemed insatiable, and I began to fear for how long I might have to endure this madness.

The drone of a car and lights from down the road caused an abrupt seizure in their coital collisions. Up 'til then, except for their muffled ecstasy, there had been only the dull syncopated roar of the waves. Now Charlotte began to whimper softly. Ned whispered not to worry, that no one would discover them. But she, to my utter and complete rapture, would not be comforted.

She urged him to finish. Though the thought of watching and hearing this spectacle come to fruition sickened me, the idea of release from the situation overwhelmed my disgust, causing me to mentally join Charlotte in her cheerleading.

In spite of his invigorated effort, however, Ned continued on for several minutes more without appearing to be any closer to our now shared goal. My anxiety grew. Sweat wetted my brow and, since I could not wipe it away, ran into my eyes, stinging them painfully. Still, Ned lumbered fitfully along like some enormous bull-seal indifferent to the pleas of his suffering mate beneath. I began to grow angry at him for both my sake and hers. How could he be so selfish? Couldn't he see that the fun had gone out of it for her? My eyes burning and my joints aching from having crouched in that awkward position for so long, I sat there for another minute until my anger at that man finally reached a boiling point and I could take it no longer. Standing bolt upright, I yelled down at him at the top of my lungs: "Either come now or give it up, you selfish son-of-a-bitch!"

As my echo died, only the distant crash of the surf came to fill its place. Even though the relief at finally breaking from the trap was monumental, I quickly realized this had been a grave error in judgment. Then a sound such as I had never heard broke forth from below me: it started like a siren, slowly and deliberately building to an almost visible apex. At its crescendo, it sounded as though a sick infant and a wounded animal had mingled their grief together into one bloodcurdling shriek. Charlotte was screaming.

Suddenly, Ned's huge featureless form loomed before me. An animal rage was palpable in the air between us. A fear such as I have never known gripped me, causing only one thought to pulse through my febrile brain: RUN AWAY! Ned, however, was blocking the only feasible route of escape with his formidable mass. It was only a matter of seconds before the commencement of the pounding of a lifetime, so I did the only thing I thought possible, rash though it was. Bending forward and crouching slightly, I lunged at him, pointing my head and left shoulder directly at his chest. As we were on a slight hill, the sheer force of the unexpected blow sent him tumbling backward onto the street.

Since Charlotte was still screeching and lights were beginning to turn on in the houses around us, I wasted no time admiring my success. Like a briefly captured, suddenly freed wild animal, I ran with mindless and panicked enthusiasm down the road. For several blocks, I kept thinking I heard Ned's footfall thudding behind me. This kept me sprinting at track-record speed and darting right and left down the various streets in an attempt to lose him. When I was too winded to go on, I stopped to listen for any sounds of pursuit. Except for my own panting, all was quiet. I set about orienting myself and saw I was only a few blocks from my hotel. I began walking to it, trying to appear as though I had merely gone for a late evening stroll.

The hotel was dark when I reached it. I quietly slipped into my room and began packing. I was not frantic, though. I decided to remain calm and leave at a reasonable hour to avoid any suspicion. After all, I thought, neither of them could have gotten a good enough look to identify me. I should act as if I'd done nothing wrong, which, since I felt I actually hadn't done anything wrong, would not be a stretch.

I finished packing, then lay on the bed to rest until the morning. I was sad that there at the end of the night I was still without my Darling. But I comforted myself with the thought that a near miss such as I'd had implied my intuition had put me on the right trail. Apparently, I was more tired than I realized because I soon fell asleep. When I woke, the light in the window betrayed it was morning.

I got up, washed my face, brushed my teeth, and changed into the clothes I'd laid out the night before. The Innkeeper had evidently heard nothing of the scene at the restaurant nor of the Ned and Charlotte episode. At least, if he had heard something, he did not make the connection or even mention it as I checked out. I was pleased by this. I wanted to leave town quietly, unhindered in the continued pursuit of my Love. Her behavior the night before made me certain she must already have fled down the coast, so I knew I must lose no time.

I was in my car headed to the highway when I was startled by the sight of Ned and Charlotte walking toward me on the same side of the street. There was no way to avoid them if they looked my way, so I quickly put on my sunglasses. As I passed them, however, it was apparent that the night before had not passed restfully for either of them. Their tired, disinterested expressions assured me I was at no risk of being discovered. I could not help laughing a little at the hapless couple. How could I have hated them so? They were perfectly harmless. In fact, I felt so confident in my cause that, as I turned south back onto Highway 1 and sped off to find my salvation, I honestly wished them well.

~

THE ROUTE SOUTH WAS CROWDED. I inched along the narrow, winding road behind awestruck tourists who gawked at the highly photographed Pacific vistas. Normally, I would have been tense and irritable in such a situation, but I remained calm on that day. I had gotten out of town without any complications and had actually seen my Love, so I felt content with whatever pace fate ordained. Even though my Darling had fled at the sight of me, I felt everything was working out wonderfully. I now knew she actually *existed*. This gave me the easy satisfaction of a man betting on a fixed fight. Everything was essentially certain. All I need do was sit back and follow wherever destiny might lead.

At first, I thought of nothing. My mind was comfortably at rest. But eventually, the tedium of staring at the back of a white Ford Taurus produced an almost hypnotic reverie. My mind drifted, and I became nostalgic over my past romantic life. I floated further back, finally casting a line into the long undisturbed pool of my first, poignant childhood romances.

Her name was Ann Robins. She had curly flaxen hair, excitable green eyes, and a mischievous, sly smile. I was in love with her for most of the first grade school year. But I was shy. I adored her from afar. During quiet drawing assignments, I would rest my face on my hand and peep through my fingers to the front of the classroom where she sat. I swooned over the slight sway of her curls as she vigorously scrawled out leaning trees, dogs at play, and busy bees all under a yellow smiling sun. At recess, I would scan the playground until I found her and would forthwith keep track of her every movement while engaged in apparent carefree play.

Then one day in the cafeteria, as we were moving through the lunch buffet line, I saw her up in front of me. After quick calculation, I realized that she would be one of the thirty students with whom I would share the table during our meal. I kept my head down as we filed into the dining hall and prayed as only an innocent child is capable that she would be at the other end of the table.

Cruel fate, of course, seated her directly opposite me. I was filled with anxiety and anguish. She already knew my thoughts, I was sure. She was ready to laugh at me as soon as I looked up from my fish sticks. All those around me were consumed with consuming their mid-day meal and were making a great hubbub while doing it. Screams, laughs, and jibes shook the hall and sent haggard lunch-duty teachers rushing from table to table to subdue the most boisterous. With so much distraction, perhaps I could observe her without being seen? Maybe she had not yet noticed me. I slowly raised my eyes from my plate to steal a look at my radiant love.

Before me she sat, completely unaware of the heart across the table that palpitated so wildly in honor of her tender beauty. She was laughing and chattering just like the rest of the magpies at the table. But she was also eating — and to my utter disgust, eating like a voracious pig. She shoveled a heaping spoonful of green peas into her demure little mouth, then laughed at Mike Stouffer who had shoved a French fry up his nose. She crammed in two fish sticks, then gazed absently about, chomping like a cow chewing its cud. She made an end of her chocolate pudding in one mouthful. Throughout the whole ordeal, her napkin lay to the right of her tray, neatly folded and untouched.

As I watched this display, I looked more closely at all the things about her that had inspired my love. Yes, her hair was still golden and beautiful. Her eyes too were the same light and lovely green. Even her smile, though cluttered with the remains of her lunch, retained a remnant of its charm. Why then did I now find her so completely unlovable? What was causing the sickness in the pit of my stomach? How had it had happened that I was out of love and enveloped in despair?

Just then, Mark Burgen, with the innate timing bestowed on all class clowns and bullies — he being the latter of the two — launched a spoon full of pudding at my face and hit his target dead-center. The sudden hush of fear and apprehension which follows all spontaneous, bold action — both glorious and unsavory — fell upon the entire table. Then, like the first glass to crash to the floor from a tottering china display case, a burst of laughter broke loose from one at the table. That one was Ann Robins.

The deluge of laughter which followed can easily be imagined. Three teachers rushed the table. One yanked the now smug and triumphant Mr. Burgen — he had threatened retribution after I'd stopped him from crowding in line for four-square — to his feet and marched him off to the office. The other two tried to restore order as I wiped my face clean with my napkin and made a poor pretense of laughing it off. Later that day, I was given two orange-flavored chewable Bayer aspirin and sent home. But the severe headache, painful though it was, was nothing compared to the sickness in my heart.

I avoided Miss Robins like the plague for the rest of the year. The combination of her pig-like manners and admittedly unintentional betrayal undermined any hope of resurrecting my previous passion. But I never considered her an enemy. I kept her at a distance so that she could remain a bittersweet reminder of the disappointment of my first love.

I did not stumble into the realm of romance again until the fifth grade, that hotbed of romantic intrigue. I, however (and as usual), had been oblivious to this intrigue 'til approximately the middle of the year. At that time, Suzanne Wonderly, the friend of pudgy Michelle Hassendorf, informed me that said friend was extremely interested in a relationship of the romantic nature with yours truly. I was at first thrown into a flutter and soon became thoroughly confused as a result of what followed.

Michelle was playing tetherball not twenty yards from where Suzanne and I sat on a bench under a trimmed weeping willow like two generals negotiating terms. The fact that

Michelle was so close and that she kept looking at me with an expectant, enamored smile on her fat little face intensified the tumult in my head and breast.

"You think she's cute, right?" demanded Suzanne.

"Well, yeah, I guess so," was my feeble reply.

"Well, she thinks you're cute, too, so what's the problem?"

I didn't know what the problem was or why I was so torn as to what to do. As I listened to Suzanne argue the case, I could see that her logic was irrefutable: if, in fact, I was attracted to Michelle, it would be completely insupportable to not take the next step and "go with her." Still, my head spun with indecision. And so, in order not to fall off the bench, I decided to focus on Suzanne's face as her chirpy voice blended with the twittering birds.

She had a very pleasant face, one that seemed particularly attractive as expressions of incredulity and reproach alternately passed over it. Watching her face, I began to relax a bit. I even began to feel affection for it. Then it happened. While focused on Suzanne's face as she grilled me like a trained interrogator, a rebel thought skipped across my synapses: "I don't like her. I like you." I was immediately shocked and appalled at the thought, but I knew it was fact. And, of course, this observation helped nothing but left me doubly confused as to what to do. My inability to cope with the circumstance allowed my thoughts to maul my conscience unmercifully. I felt there must be something wrong in the fact that I felt like I did. How could it be right that I had thought Michelle was cute, completely ignoring Suzanne, only to suddenly and unexpectedly take notice of and fall for Suzanne? It was illogical. It was unfair. But, much to my chagrin, it *was*.

I was gazing at her unguardedly, continuing against my will to think she had a lovely little face, when Suzanne stopped talking. A thin, knowing smile played on her lips. This smile, coupled with her sudden silence, alarmed me. Had she read my mind? I felt the quick heat of my blushing face. This evidently confirmed what she had suspected. Her eyes glimmered like a savage who, on the serendipitous discovery of its prey, silently prepares to make the kill. I watched her lips — pink and moist — as, slowly, they began to part. I felt sick and weak in my stomach. She was going to say something, and I dreaded it. She was going to tell me she liked me. She was going to say she and I should "go together." But how I was going to respond, I wasn't sure of at all. And I didn't wait to find out. I leaped from the bench and ran with blinding speed to the boys' bathroom.

The cool, tiled bathroom acted like a balm on my disturbed mind. I began to consider my situation. Possibly I could stay in the bathroom for the rest of my grade year? Maybe the universe would collapse and save me from having to make any decision? Just then, the class dolt, Marty Stokes, came in picking his nose.

"Suzanne says she likes you and wants to know if you like her," he said bluntly while absently unzipping his pants. He then walked to the urinal and began to relieve himself.

I said nothing, but began to pace back and forth. Marty let nature take its course and appeared completely unintrigued by my situation. I wondered what to do. What was right in such a situation? I did think Suzanne was cute, but did I want to go with her? And what about poor Michelle? How would she take it if her supposed best friend, the emissary of her feelings, and I began to "go together." Wouldn't she be crushed beyond repair? Wouldn't I be destroying an innocent young girl by callously throwing her over for her best friend? After another minute or so Marty zipped up his pants and turned to me with a stupid look of expectation on his face.

"Tell her I'm contemplating infinity."

I'd said it before I knew what I was going to say.

Marty gave the comment not one moment's thought. He turned and walked out without a word. I listened for what kind of response this answer would get. I heard nothing. Moments later, Marty ambled back in with a blank expression on his face and stated:

"She says she wants to know what that means."

I sent him out without an answer and waited until the bell for class sounded. When it finally rang, I waited a few minutes more. I decided being late for my class, which neither Suzanne nor Michelle were in, was better than making this decision. When I left the bathroom, the whole of the vast playground was empty. Everything was quiet. As I walked to my class, I kept expecting Michelle and Suzanne to leap out from around a corner and jump on me while chanting in unison:

"Her or me? Her or me? Her or me?"

I did not, however, meet up with either of them. I went to my class and got scolded by the teacher for being late. When I went out for the next recess, Suzanne and Michelle played two-square together, ignoring me completely. I was glad to have been relieved of my decision at first and went about playing as usual. Since I hadn't been friends with either of them and we played different games at recess, it was not difficult to avoid them.

But after a few days (their interest in me having never renewed itself), I found myself unexpectedly disappointed. Although I knew by that time that I hadn't wanted to "go with" either of them, I was still bothered that they had so easily given up on me. It seemed strange, and I could never seem to get over it. From then on, no matter how much a girl professed to be in love with me, I always secretly watched her for that moment of disillusionment. If I didn't detect it, I would question and analyze her in my mind and soon discover that I was disenchanted. And that was essentially where I had stayed until I had set out for my Love.

∼

THEY CAME IN THROUGH A SMALL CRACK IN THE WINDOW. I discovered it later while replenishing the cracker crumbs to keep them coming. I had been lying on the bed in the dimly-lit motel room for countless hours when I saw the first one. At first, I thought my eyes were playing tricks on me again. There had been so many little flicks and glimmers on the walls over the past few days. But, after a few moments, I realized the little black dot must be alive. As it made its way down the wall to the carpet, it seemed a goal was involved. Very soon, another one came, poking its way tentatively along just as the other had. The first one had reached the halfway point by that time. After another minute, it disappeared into what must have seemed a jungle. An hour later, a whole line of them was marching the same crooked path to the carpet, then returning with their load of cracker crumb from the table up to the small crack in the window.

    I lay listlessly watching them for another hour or so before I got the idea. The first day I arrived at the garish Madonna Inn near San Luis Obisbo I discovered a little daddy longlegs. I had been in the room awhile, lying on my stomach with my head hanging over the side of the bed, when I saw him. He was sitting patiently in his whispery-thin web in the corner. I wondered at first if he wasn't dead, so I gently poked his web. He only tensed up. But when I poked at him again, he made a showy display by whirling himself about violently. He was so small I could have crushed his whole body with the tip of my pinkie, leaving only his legs to sprawl out a few tenths of an inch. Yet, he was willing to stand his ground. Such bravado from this little speck of a spider engendered such an affection in me for him that I almost cried. I watched him obsessively for the rest of the day, wondering how he had been able to survive there with such an apparent poverty of prey. By the next day, I had forgotten the whole episode, but the ants reminded me of him.

    I rolled over to see if he was still there. He sat in his web, stoically waiting for whatever providence might provide him.

When I saw him, I nearly yelped with joy. Jumping off the bed in the heartiest display of energy I had made for five days, I leaped over to the line of ants going up and down the wall. I gently pinched one of them from its path so as not to crush it. I then jumped back over the bed to where the tiny predator awaited the sacrifice I was about to give him. The ant stuck to my fingers at first, as if it knew somehow what was about to happen. I was finally able to flick it lightly from the open palm of my hand across which it was aimlessly roaming. It lit an inch or so from the spider, causing the web to quiver. At this motion in his web, the spider tensed up as he had before. But when the ant continued its struggling, the spider was on it in a spasmodic burst.

Seizing it abruptly, he pulled the ant to him and began to fill it with his venom. The ant continued to struggle to free itself from the grasp of the spider. But eventually, it stopped. The spider then began delicately twirling it with his front legs, covering his victim with a silky web his rear legs brought forth from his tiny hindquarters. The dainty, deliberate movements the little spider was now exhibiting fascinated me. His motions were both efficient and rhythmic. They had an almost meditative quality to them. His legs moved in perfect harmony with one another, spinning the increasingly covered ant so smoothly that it seemed as though he was dancing with it. This seemed at first to contrast with the predatory aggression he'd displayed only moments before. But after watching him turn and spin the ant a bit longer, I realized that the certainty of his instinct and the precision with which he brought it off were evident in both the careful process he was now using, as well as the more aggressive one of before. I dropped several more ants into his web just to watch him in action and noticed the light fading in the room only after it became almost too dark to see.

⁓

Around that time, I heard what sounded like a low moan coming through the wall. Something disturbing about the sound frightened me, pulling my attention away from the spider. Silence gathered in the stillness like water in a tidal pool. Shadows hung on the walls and crouched in the corners of the darkening room. I sprang up and stuck my ear to the wall to listen more closely for another sound like the one I'd just heard. When I heard it again, my heart jumped to my throat. I was sure now that it was a woman moaning. And she sounded as though she might be in pain. I became anxious and afraid about what might be happening to this young woman that would make her moan so. Such an ungodly sound. I felt obliged to make sure there was no foul play involved. I pressed my ear to the wall again. That was when I heard the man groan. He sounded as though he might be in pain as well. I pulled my ear from the wall in fear of hearing more. In the sick world through which I was roaming, it seemed thoroughly conceivable that someone was torturing some innocent young man and woman in the next room.

But just as I was struggling with whether or not to take action and call the police to save this hapless young couple, I heard both of them moan in unison. And the quality of this dual moan made the nature of what was happening in the room next door all too apparent. I fell back from the wall onto the bed, sick to my stomach to think I had been unwittingly eavesdropping on some overzealous newlywed couple. I stared at the crumbling stucco ceiling for several minutes. I felt inexplicably stunned. But then I felt a slow bitterness and anger rising up in me. Here I was trying in good faith to find my Love, that apex of happiness, and fate saw fit to rub my nose in some plebeian romp in the hay.

Now I started to see what was taking place next door as just that. They probably weren't a couple at all. They were probably both cheating on someone in this vulgar, ostentatious motel. Most likely, they had met in some dark, seedy bar that had only beer advertisements for decoration and had recognized in each other a mutual contempt for all that was good in life. Meanwhile, their faithful mates sat at home, alone, waiting for them to return. The unfairness of the situation became unbearable to me. I was just about to pack my bags to get away from the obscenity taking place next door to me when I heard another groan from the woman. My fuse had already burned to the quick, and the breath it took that young harlot to moan was just enough to fan the flame and finish it off.

"Why don't you shut up, you fucking whore!" I screamed. "Can't you see that not everyone wants to be part of your sick and demented sex life?"

Silence washed over everything. I felt a sudden, smug

satisfaction at this response. I had showed them. I wasn't going to sit by idly and let them live their lives of corruption right under my nose. After quiet had reigned another minute, I calmly started the process of packing my bags. This was rather involved as I had allowed the room to become quite untidy over the past five days. I told the manager on my arrival to have the housekeeping crew deliver a fresh batch of towels and bedding each day, but not to come into my room or even knock on my door. I gave him several hundred dollars so he would see to my request, which he had. As a result, clothes were strewn everywhere, hanging from chairs and lamps, and were mixed in with heaps of used towels and bedding. I began digging through the mess. Clothes and linens swished through the air as I threw them into separate piles. Fortunately, it did not take long to divide them and shortly after I had begun, I was ready to start filling my bags.

The whole time I had been doing this I listened closely for any sound from next door and had heard nothing. But as I actually began to pack, I thought I heard something again. I leaped up on the bed and stuck my ear to the wall in an effort to catch them at their little subterfuge. What I heard, however, did not sound like what I had heard before. It sounded, instead, like muffled sobs. I pushed my ear even closer to the wall in an effort to discern if this noise was in fact the sound of someone crying. After a minute or so, I was sure it was sobs I was hearing.

This reaction caught me off guard. I had felt sure I was dealing with hardened people who could care less about the condemnation of anyone, let alone some nut in a room next to them. I had just wanted to stop them from being so vocal. It disturbed me to think I was the cause of this woman's unhappiness. I wanted to do something to make her stop crying. Paltry though it was, I decided an apology was the best I had to offer. But I figured they were probably still naked and that if I went to her room, she would have to dress in a hurry, which would be even more upsetting. Maybe I could just send a note through the manager. I had *him* in my hip pocket; he would do it without question. I put my ear to the wall again while trying to figure out how to get her my apology. She was still sobbing. I became desperate to make her stop. So I finally made a decision. I got right next to the wall and yelled as loud as I could:

"I'm really sorry. I don't really think you're a whore!"

As soon as I'd said it, I felt much better. In fact, I became downright enthused about making the best apology I could under the circumstances; so I added in a booming, yet still conciliatory voice:

"Hey, really, don't even worry about it. I've had sex with women who were much louder than you!"

Again, silence returned. I pushed my ear to the wall to check out the situation. I heard nothing. I took this lack of sound as a good sign, which sent a flood of relief over me. I hadn't realized how much I had vested in making this unknown woman feel better. My apparent success made me happy. I finished packing my bags, feeling good about my apology and thinking things would surely have to start going my way.

A sharp knock on my door came just as I closed my suitcase. As I walked to the door, I wondered if it could be the woman coming to say she had forgiven me for my outburst. I knew this was unlikely, but I did actually hope to see her standing there when I opened the door. Instead of a woman, however, I found a familiar-looking muscular young man wearing tan slacks and a scowl. This was disappointing, but, despite his grimace, I decided to maintain a good attitude.

"Can I help you?" I said affably.

Without a word, he pulled his arm back behind him as though he were about to pitch a baseball. What he delivered when his arm came forward, however, was not a baseball, but a clinched fist which struck me square on the jaw and sent me flying back onto the floor. I lay there stunned, then looked up to see my unknown attacker in silhouette stepping into my room. He loomed over me for another moment, still only a shadowy menace, then bent down and seized me by the shirt. He yanked me up sharply to receive another of his fists, this time directly in the face. I felt blood gush from my poor smashed nose. The blood running over my lips reminded me that I bleed easily. Even as a child, when I skinned my knee or accidentally cut myself with a pocket knife, the wound always bled buckets before I could get it to stop. When my attacker pulled me up for yet another blow, I wondered briefly about how long I would bleed this time before it stopped. My head had fallen to the side, so the expected thud landed on my ear. By that point, I felt no pain, and I only felt where it landed.

Now, though I had only been struck three times, they were decidedly well-landed blows. This, I think, (when coupled with the fact that over the last few weeks, as I have said, I hadn't been eating well and was weak as a result anyway) was the reason I began to lose consciousness. I was anxious about this because I knew I was losing consciousness, but I wasn't sure my attacker did. So I was worried he might continue to beat me a bit longer, possibly even breaking bones in the process, before he understood I was unconscious. You might wonder how I could think all this in such a small period of time, but remember that the brain is an amazing thing. It can appraise a situation much more quickly than we can articulate that appraisal.

In any event, my fear was unwarranted because he did not hit me again. He only jerked me up by the shirt and let me dangle a moment. I did sense he was weighing whether or not to continue the beating. But in the end, he dropped me to the ground and just stood there. Even though my consciousness was still flagging, and I knew I should probably lie there motionless, I couldn't help it: I wanted to get a look at my assailant. I rolled my head over to find him glaring down at me. And to my complete surprise, I recognized him as that phony prick who sat next to me with his wife in the restaurant in Carmel. Evidently, he recognized me too, because a smile of contempt broke across his face.

We remained in our respective positions appraising one another several moments more. I did not try to mask my feelings but obstinately returned his look of contempt. Why he did not recommence pummeling me, I do not know. He could see what I thought of him. But, after glancing around my room with scorn, he again smiled at me contemptuously, then turned and left. I lay there a while looking at the bedspread hanging next to me. My nose continued to bleed as I wondered at its hideous rust and gold floral pattern. Why was it that cheap things seem always to be done in such poor taste? Was the person who designed this bedspread not aware of how ugly it was when they designed it? Maybe they knew but just didn't care because they weren't getting paid enough to try to make it look good.

When my nose stopped bleeding, I reached over and used the bedspread to wipe myself as clean as I cared to be for the moment. I then stood up — not an easy task as my head was still reeling and began to throb as soon as I was upright. I decided to bite the bullet and get out as quickly as I could. This whole episode was yet another sign to me. I had been too long off the trail of my Love. Feelings of disappointment at missing her on the beach had seeped into my mind and resurrected doubts. I soon felt sorry for myself and had come to this place to hide from my destiny. So I knew this whipping was not from that superficial, piece-of-shit yuppie, but from a divine source: I had once again let myself be worn down by outside influences.

And yet, I was not ready to try again. I was still tired and the load was too heavy to pick up, let alone carry. I wasn't even sure I could ever lift it again. I was weak, and I knew it.

I grew afraid of the power following me, trying to force me forward to my Love. I wanted to escape it. I had tried in this motel, but it had found me. I grabbed my things and ran to my car. I didn't even stop to pay my bill. Fuck'em. They had my credit card number. In a matter of minutes, I was on the highway running hopelessly away.

∼

"The Whaler" wasn't crowded: Mike, the bartender; two working class fishermen muttering to one another in a corner at one end; a balding middle-age man — hair sprouting from his nose and ears — in a rumpled business suit and glasses with a big-haired, heavily made-up young woman drinking in rapt silence several tables from the fishermen; and a stoic, shriveled old man at the opposite end of the bar drinking Chivas Regal at the rate of three an hour, apparently oblivious to all around him. I'd stopped at this place just north of Ventura because my head felt too light to drive. I thought a rest and a drink or two might help calm me. Initially, I'd been put off by this dank, gloomy place and was going to leave after my first drink. But something about the dark little bar began to make me feel safe.

I had been there about an hour or so, downing rum and Coke at fifteen minute intervals. When Mike set my next drink in front of me, I suddenly felt talkative. I began to elaborate on the beauteous nature of my sweet foe, as well as on our ineluctable triumph in love, though I still did not really believe what I was saying. Mike stood behind the bar drying glasses with a dirty dishtowel. Though his hands were the picture of mobility and action, his face wore the abject, indifferent expression of some steppe-bound Russian peasant gazing at the plow horse in front of him. But I talked on anyway. His indifference seemed to represent both the indifference of the world at large and the doubt I was fighting within myself. I talked and talked, but believed no more than Mike appeared to.

After going on for another half an hour, I heard the old man let out a short puff of air in apparent scorn. I saw him looking at me in the mirror, shaking his head. He then turned away but continued to shake his head slightly. This little display both annoyed and intrigued me.

"Hey, Mike, what's that old man's story?" I asked.

Mike glanced down at him, then back to me.

"He comes here every day," he said apathetically. "I think he got fired from his job at the University."

The old man suddenly spat, then snarled, "Tenure, you ignorant clod. I lost my tenure, then I quit! Nobody fired me."

Other than the word "another," he had uttered nothing. In fact, before his little outburst, I had wondered if he had gone to sleep between orders, so quiet was he. Now that I knew he had been listening, however, and given Mike's indifference, I felt like talking to him. I wanted to see if he would vocalize my doubt, and, if he did, to walk into the arms of it and let it engulf me completely. I picked up my drink, ambled down, and sat on the stool next to him.

He did not look at me when I sat down but continued to regard himself in the mirror. I stared at him a moment and even made a face to see if he would respond. I got nothing for my effort. Finally, I decided to go the direct route.

"What do you think, old man?" I demanded sarcastically. "I know you've been listening. You seem skeptical about what I've been saying here. So why don't you tell me if I'll find her, my Darling, I mean?"

"Not likely," he said flatly without looking at me.

I could see he felt this way before he'd spoken, but his quick response surprised, even frightened me a little. Still, I could not resist questioning him further. He seemed so sure. I wanted to know why.

"What do you mean?" I asked, smiling and trying to appear confident, though I felt my expression betrayed my uncertainty.

"What's wrong with me, gramps?" I forced myself to continue. "Why don't I deserve what I've been looking for so hard?"

"Why did the monkey come down from the tree?" he asked abruptly in an arched, sardonic tone as he turned and glared at me.

"What?" I stammered, taken off guard by the venomous way he had asked.

"Wrong, you pathetic little drone, not 'What?' but 'Why?' To ask 'Why?' That's why the monkey came down from the tree."

"What are you talking about?" I asked, confused and growing a little angry. "I was asking why you thought I wouldn't find my Love, who I will find, by the way, in spite of whatever you might say."

I was surprised to find myself believing the last part of what

I said more than I had been able to only moments before.

"You're impetuous," he said sharply, turning away from me again. Then, as he slowly lifted his whisky up to his taut little mouth, he said with deliberation, "You are a misappropriator of significance, and your temerity will be your ruin."

I felt the false, forced smile I'd been wearing drain from my face. I watched him shoot down his drink. The buzz I had developed began to fade. I grabbed onto the bar to steady myself and called out, "We'll need a couple more drinks down here, Mike."

Face forward, I watched the old man in the mirror. After Mike brought our drinks and returned to the other end of the bar, the old man spoke again.

"You're wondering how I can say this to you, a young man I don't even know," he started in a thin, whispery undertone, his eyes sparkling with contempt. "You're thinking I might be crazy. But you are afraid I might be right, aren't you?"

He caught my eye in the mirror.

"Yes, I can see the flicker of fear there in your eyes."

I felt a slight shudder run through me. He laughed softly, then turned his wrinkled face full on me, looking me straight in the eye. A low hum began in my brain. I felt I was falling into a trance. I think I even drooled a little. I tottered on my barstool. But the old man's stare seemed to hold me in place.

"Do you want to know who to blame for you not getting your 'Darling girl'?" he hissed at me, the corners of his lips curling into a wicked little smile. "Do you want to hear, my little man?"

I shook my head up and down mechanically like a child responding to a magician.

"Blame Moses," he said with a quick puff of air, "blame Socrates," he said, raising his index finger up in front of my face, "or Jesus or Aristotle or whomever you can identify as the one who conceived of human beings as creatures separate from the animals. Whomever you would hold culpable of making that proposition acceptable to those who have shaped the Western World is the guilty party."

I sat still, numbed, staring at him. He was silent but continued to fix me with his intense, steady gaze.

"I have seen you before and continue to see you every day," he began again, "throughout history, and in all the people today who are just like you. Reckless egotism, mean-spirited in its blind self-pursuit, was and is the most high God. This is the only God which is not, nor will ever be, dead. And this God truly possesses what all other Gods were supposed to have had: the power to destroy the human race, and possibly the world."

"But I still pity the poor human being," he said after a pause, in which he had turned away from me and downed the shot of whisky Mike had placed in front of him. "It seems that, in the end, this pathetic little animal exists for the sole purpose of chasing its tail, stopping only occasionally to wonder why it does so."

We sat in silence, me staring at him and him appearing to stare at the nothing between the bottles behind the bar. For a little while, my mind struggled and gasped under the things he had said. Then I stopped resisting, and I began to float. Soon, I broke through the surface of my stupor and began to breathe and go over his words. I had long ago thought or read most of them. Of course I had. In fact, was I not pursuing my goal (my sacred, albeit as yet unidentified, Love) because of these very things? In order to fly into the face of all he'd said and more? I must have been really drunk to have let him get me all worked up like that.

But looking over at him — the wildness I saw coming from his eyes even in profile — I couldn't help it; he made me feel odd. I knew the things he had said were rehashed, bloated pontifications stewed in and spewed out of his hopeless oblivion. He obviously saw himself as some sort of misunderstood prophet, martyred by contemporary indifference. But there was still something unnerving about this old man and his way of putting even threadbare clichés. Something I had to explore further. I decided to quiz him in hope that something he might say would point me in the direction of my goal, my Love, which I felt surging urgently back up inside me. But he spoke before I could.

"You have only one chance," he said. "Only one chance, if you can accept it. And I don't think you can."

"What is it?" I blurted out without thinking. "Tell me, please!"

Again he studied my face for a minute, then solemnly spoke the following:

"Hear this now, for here is wisdom: there is only one answer to all eternal questions," he paused, leaving the incomplete thought dangling mid-air between us… then, with punctuated deliberation, he said: "I don't know."

I waited, expecting something more. He said nothing.

"'I don't know?'" I parroted.

"Exactly."

"What do you mean 'I don't know?' What the hell kind of answer is that?" I demanded with a vehemence that surprised even me.

He said nothing.

Then suddenly, I felt the tightness slowly unravel in my chest. After a few more moments, I felt overwhelmed, enraptured by a boundless sense of relief. I began to smile. Then I started to laugh.

"That's it," I finally said through my laughter. "Your big gem of truth is 'I don't know.' You fucking loon. I've wondered about myself, but, Jesus, you really take the cake, you bitter old fucking lost-yer-tenure nut!"

I laughed and shook my head, then laughed some more. At the start, the old man appeared to be taken a little off guard and seemed slightly ruffled. But the next minute, he stared indifferently at his drink. I kept on laughing helplessly. I yelped. I pointed at him. I howled and hooted. For some reason, his indifference now exacerbated things. Before, he'd had me stupefied; now he had me laughing with mindless abandon.

After another minute, however, I stopped laughing abruptly. At first, I didn't understand what had happened. I saw the old man sitting there, and I wanted to keep laughing at him. But the wind had been crushed from my lungs. I was being dragged off my barstool. I glanced in the mirror and saw Mike's fuzzy arm around my neck, his unshaven, still stony face hovering over my shoulder. The next thing I knew, I was on the ground outside the bar. Mike stood over me wearing a fierce expression. I blinked up at him in confusion while trying to catch my breath.

"I've had enough of you," he said truculently. "Stay the fuck out of here, or I'm going to give you more than the fucking fat lip you've got already. You got me, you little fuck?"

He turned and slammed the door behind him, leaving me on the pavement next to my car. I sat there in a daze. But, after I caught my breath, I became incensed at what had just happened. Who the fuck was that low rent, son-of-a-bitch of a bartender to treat me like that? I felt like going in and tearing him apart. I paced back and forth by my car for ten full minutes, cussing and fuming at the unfairness and indignity of what I had just suffered, trying to hatch a plan to serve deadpan Mike his head on a platter.

But then it all came disturbingly together. Mike, like the yuppie before him, was merely an instrument. My destiny had done this to me, I was sure. I sat down on the ground next to my Beauty and put my head in my hands. I would never be able to escape it. I could see that. I might not believe in my mission, but my destiny would never forget. And it would continue to subject me to such battering and abuse whenever I went astray.

Tears of self-pity began to run down my face. I felt oppressed.

Why must *I* suffer this way? Why must *I* be the one to save my Darling? For a moment, I even hated her (though I confessed it instantly). I thought of rejecting it all and running away again, but I knew that was useless. My fate would find me wherever I went.

After a while, when I had exhausted myself with frustration and resentment, a calm came over me. I gazed up at the vast empty sky. And, like a shockwave hitting then passing through me, I was overwhelmed with reverence for the power in control of my life. It was amazing. It was awe-inspiring. I recalled my previous declarations. I remembered the fervor with which I thought I had believed. But this time was different. Never was I so sure of what I was doing before that moment. A smile of satisfaction, of unshakable conviction settled onto my face.

"All right, you win, " I shouted out to the cloudless, blue sky. "I will not forget again! I will not waver, and I will not relent! I will return to the path and will not leave it until I have found her!"

I sprang up and over to my car as though it were my victory chariot and tore out of the parking lot. My cause was never more sure to me. There would be no more doubts. There would be no more uncertainty. I had been beaten into submission. I believed with the full capacity of my being. I would serve my fate like a faithful slave until I had fulfilled my purpose in life and saved my Love and myself or died trying.

PART III

THE SEARCH ENDS

I BARRELED DOWN THE REMAINDER OF HIGHWAY 1 and burst out onto the LA freeway system. My Love had continued to elude me. So I was again forced to ask the same questions. Where would she be? How could I find her in this maze of people and lights? Fueled by frustration from a lack of answers, I drove like a cat with its tail on fire. The people I passed seemed to not even notice me, in spite of my crazed driving. Just another microbe flitting through the soup of their reality. But they were as irrelevant to me as I was to them. The only ones who concerned me were my Darling (the guiding light for my storm-darkened mind) and the CHP. And the last only bothered me intermittently as they pinballed around in the rear of my mind.

My hotel room lay in the distance, waiting for me like a lair. I must get there. I must get there. To plan. To scheme. To work out where she is. All this and more sucking and swirling in my mind. The problem was how to get there through this tangle of freeway. I had called when I'd reached Santa Barbara to get directions to the Beverly-Wilshire Hotel (my Platinum

Card representative had suggested this place and had patched me through for directions after making the reservations). But the directions were on the back of a random scrap of paper which now lay somewhere among Snicker's wrappers, Coke cans, a half-empty bottle of Jack Daniel's, a Harper's magazine, wadded up underwear, sweat-stained tourist T-shirts, and myriad other sundry items strewn over the interior of the car. All I could remember was the freeway number: 405. I didn't worry about it for too long, though. The muse that had led me so well thus far would guide me in the end.

I slowed the Beauty after taking the split to the 405 in order to try to find the exit, but I didn't fare well in spite of that. Initially, I was on the lookout for Wilshire Blvd. and so paid close attention to every sign. But I soon got distracted checking out the people in cars next to me. Apparently, what I was doing was not common. Almost no one actually looked around to observe the horde with whom they shared the freeways. Occasionally, some kid in the back of a mini-van would give me a blank stare. I started sticking my tongue out at them, just to see if I could get some sort of reaction. Nada. I started to wonder if maybe they were drugged. Maybe the child pornography industry had come up with the perfect means of transporting their kidnap victims/latest stars from hiding place to set, then back again. What a brilliant ruse, I thought. Parent type in the front of a typical family vehicle, child in perfect view: who would suspect?

As I was pondering this, one of these little shits flipped me off. Unprovoked in any way by me, this tow-headed little bastard just flew me a bird. This really pissed me off. What the hell is happening in this world, I thought, when kids acted like this without provocation? I pulled up next to the mother and began gesticulating wildly to get her attention to let her know what kind of little asshole she had given birth to. The stony side of her face was all I got. The kid reveled in this and kept making lewd gestures. I started honking my horn, hoping this might somehow bring her to life. Still, nothing. I then wondered if maybe she wasn't his mother at all, but rather some automaton built for efficient transport of rich, obnoxious children whose parents didn't want to deal with them either.

I was considering swerving at her when she took an exit off the freeway. I looked up in time to see the Wilshire Blvd. exit sign. She had made an erratic cut to the exit, and a car was right on my ass, so I couldn't make it over in time. I watched dumbstruck as that little fucker made a mocking face while signaling good-bye with the international "up yours" gesture. I screamed and cursed, though I knew it was futile. So, still fuming from this maddening exchange, I took the next exit, which actually led to another freeway.

I drove on for a short time, passing several exits before deciding to get off to make a call to the hotel for new directions. I continued south for a bit through a tattered, worn neighborhood 'til I found a gas station with a phone. When I described where I was to the concierge (to whom the registration desk had passed me), he told me to remain calm and not show any fear to anyone walking by. I thought this a strange thing to say, but then I thought maybe my voice sounded edgy after my recent experience. Still, his patronizing approach annoyed me. I told him I was calm and to just tell me how to get to his fucking hotel. He tried to explain them to me several times, but I was tired and kept making mistakes when repeating the directions back to him.

Finally, he told me he would like to send someone out to retrieve me. Normally I would have taken offense at such a suggestion, but I was feeling frazzled. I told him to send two people as I didn't want to bother with driving anymore. I said not to worry, as there would be a fat tip in it for him, as well as my rescuers. He seemed to grow stiff at the suggestion of a tip, but I ignored his tone, told him I'd be waiting, and hung up the phone.

Approximately an hour later, a muscular blonde young man dressed in a spiffy red, gold-trimmed uniform woke me with several sharp raps on my window. I opened the door and fell out on the ground. Finishing that bottle of whisky rather than taking a little nip to help calm my nerves had probably been imprudent. The bell captain and his valet handled me with gentle alacrity, however, whisking me away to the regal, yet nonetheless sterile Beverly-Wilshire hotel. The registration process was a blur of obsequious smiles and obligatory signatures, after which I was led by the hand and safely installed in the plush bed in my thirty-five hundred dollars a night suite. After they left, I felt sick but was too tired to go to the bathroom. I vomited off to the side of my bed, took a drink out of the glass of water the bell captain had set at my bedside, then fell into an unsatisfactory sleep.

∽

I SLEPT THROUGH TO THE NEXT MORNING. When I woke, the light of day was thinly framing the curtains, and the vomit by my bed was gone. On a tray in its place was a lavish continental breakfast with fruit and pastries and a steaming pot of coffee. There were even some Tylenol caplets there for me. I did not know whether I had left orders for these things to be done, whether I had woken and called down to request them, or whether the hotel simply operated with eerie, omniscient efficiency. And just then, I didn't care. I was starving and more than a little hungover.

When I finished, I got up and stood a long time under the water in the enormous tiled shower. I considered my circumstances and options while the hot water, streaming from the shower heads facing each other, flowed over my suffering body. But the more I thought, the less I knew. I was in the middle of this vast, chaotic place without a clue as to where to recommence my search. I felt she was there, but I could not think of how to deduce where she might be. This vexed me for the majority of my shower, which, between me standing and sitting intermittently, lasted for well over an hour. In the end, I remembered that I had planned none of the things (other than the basic decision to find my Darling and my rudimentary itinerary) that ultimately put me on her trail. I realized I should dispense once and for all with trying to plan anything around locating her. I needed to trust both my intuition and fate to bring us together. This issue settled for the last time, I dressed and called to have my car brought around. I was pleasantly surprised to see the management had washed it, cleaned the interior, and gassed it up for me. I tipped the valet a hundred, then pulled out and headed west on Wilshire Blvd.

It was mid-morning by this time, and the Los Angeles day was in full swing. People were on the streets going in and out of shops and office buildings. Cars went zipping by as I cruised along unhurriedly. The traffic on the broad thoroughfare of Wilshire moved smoothly, which pleased me for some reason. I was feeling good. I had the roof off and the breeze was refreshing me more and more as I drove along. I did not turn off onto any other streets. I followed the road to wherever it was taking me. After several miles, I passed under a freeway and saw by a sign that I was in Santa Monica. Other than having heard the name before, this meant nothing to me.

When the road ended at the ocean, I had to make a decision to go north or south. But this did not annoy me. In fact, quite pleased, I simply turned south without a thought. I continued floating like this for another hour. Though relaxed, I kept on the lookout. True to the cliché about LA, there were scores of beautiful women at which one could look. It was like some huge machine somewhere was spitting them out at a designated rate per hour. They all seemed impervious to the searching stares I gave them. Even though I felt sure I would know my Love the instant I saw her, I didn't want her to slip by and delay our union because of inattention on my part. Of course, again — yet again — none of these women were her.

I also noticed the homeless on the street again. But seeing them in L.A. was different, somehow, than in San Francisco. They were pretty much everywhere, as before, but they did not make me feel so anxious. The sun was shining, and they even appeared content as they sat on a bench or by some building. A lot of them seemed to congregate by the beach. With ocean breezes to cool them and beautiful vistas and women to look at, it did not appear such a bad life.

I drove a while longer, then turned around to retrace my route back. The return trip to the hotel was as uneventful as the one away, which depressed me a bit. Although I had tried to go out with no expectations, I suppose I had hoped for something more than a smooth, hassle-free drive. When I got back to the hotel, I went straight to the bar to have some lunch. Although I had done nothing for the past few hours, I was very hungry. I ordered a turkey sandwich on rye with French fries and sucked on a huge freezing-cold frothy beer while waiting for the food to come.

Instead of thinking of my circumstance, I observed the clientele in the bar. Before long, I decided they were one of the scariest groups of people I had ever seen. Some of them moved so fluidly and dressed with such fashionable elegance and were so stereotypically beautiful. Strange though it was to picture, these human beings were actually animals who took shits and fucked. It felt almost sacrilegious even to think it. Of course, they weren't all seamless. Some of them were fat and hideously ugly. They tried to conceal it all with glamorous clothes and make-up and plastic surgery. But their efforts only succeeded in accentuating the very things they were trying to hide.

One thing they all seemed to participate in was the observation of hushed tones. No voices were raised. Not by the guests. Not by the hotel employees. Not by any of them. As I noted this, I could not help laughing at the thought of the spectacle I must have made coming in there the day before. Like most people, I tend to stumble and fall when I'm drunk. But I always insist on going on my own power whenever possible. That had been the case the day before. I recalled the stares I received as the bell captain and the valet hovered close while I tottered through the lobby. I munched on my sandwich, devoured my French fries and reveled in the idea that I had upset the workings of this smooth, whispering social order.

Turning my attention back to the central cause in my life, I asked my server to bring me a map of the greater Los Angeles areas and a large red felt-tipped marker. I intended to follow my gut instincts, but I decided I wanted to have an idea with regards to the general direction I would take each day and night. A map was soon in front of me and I was pouring over it. The opportunities in terms of direction based on freeways alone seemed almost limitless. Then there were the surface streets, most of which I was sure were not even included on this map.

This multitude of possibilities did not upset or unnerve me, though. In fact, I loved the idea of jumping mindlessly into the tangled heap of humanity this swirl of highways and byways represented. After studying the map for a while at my table, I whisked it and my unfinished beer up to my room to chart my itinerary for the evening. I already had an idea about going west again and wanted to see which options were available to me.

The afternoon sun was coming through the open curtains, throwing a weak and hazy yellow light into my room. I barely noticed the bed had been made and the room put in order. I put the map on the table to study it further. A route presented itself. I considered it based on the time it would likely consume in driving it alone, without stopping to consider any rest or eating. My calculations were based on my recent trip. No. It would take too long, even without traffic, which I could not possibly hope for given the waning hour of the afternoon. I considered another route, this time more to the north. But this proved fruitless as well. It wouldn't take enough time. I might end up back at the hotel before nine. Of course, that was far too early. My Darling would not have gone back out by then.

It struck me then that I should probably just stay in my room. I could wait for traffic to die down, have dinner and maybe a drink or two, then head out to some clubs later. Yes. That was the way to do it. Rest up some more. I had had a rough week. In fact, I was still sore from the thrashing that prick had given me the day or two before. Thank god I had covered my face quickly. He had only managed to fatten my lip, the asshole.

The rest I'd received on my body. After my drive that morning with all that sitting topped off with residual hangover, I was aching all over. That was when I remembered the health spa on the premises. Maybe I should just get myself a little massage. Nice relaxing hands soothing my bruised muscles. I liked the idea. I had nearly decided when the drink I'd ordered from room service arrived.

"Your Long Island iced tea, sir."

"Ah, David, it's so refreshing to see that such precision service still exists in a world such as ours."

I took the drink and handed a fifty to the same guy who had accompanied the bell captain to pick me up.

"Thank you, sir!" he said, beaming a perfect Colgate smile at me.

He was around my age, so it felt a little strange at first to have him calling me "sir." But I just let him anyway and had now gotten used to it. I had dealt with him several times since I'd gotten there, and we'd been getting more familiar. In remembering my experience at The Fairmont - where I had missed my Darling by not having an inside connection - I decided to try to cultivate one here right away. David, as a result, had been tipped liberally at even the most trivial of exchanges during my short time there.

"Say," I asked, looking at him in a conspiratorial way, though just why I could not have said, "how does a guy get a massage around here?"

Here, in spite of the fact that I had been encouraging

familiarity, David did something that threw me. His smile became a lascivious sneer, then he stepped backwards a bit into the corridor and looked first left then right. He then stepped back to me, but got closer than he'd been before.

"Tell you what," he said with raised eyebrows and in a much more familiar tone than he had been using before, "if you want something a little more than a massage, I can arrange it... *real* easy."

At first, I did not follow him. I guess I had had too much to drink or was maybe still tired, but I really had no idea what he might be suggesting. But I didn't let on. I just raised my glass up and took a sip from my drink without changing my expression. He evidently interpreted my pause as a different type of uncertainty than it actually was, because he winked then continued:

"No need to worry, my friend. Mum's the word and nothing but the highest quality here, I assure you. She will be incredible."

The word "she" stuck me like the LA county pandering log book dropped from a lofty height. My drink slipped from my hand, and my mouth dropped open with it. In turn, David's face fell from a wily confident smile to a look of panicked uncertainty.

"Mr. Askew," he stammered. "I hope I haven't... I mean, I really thought you meant... oh, Mr. Askew, please tell me I haven't offended you."

His face was now warped into an agonized expression. I regained some of my composure but was still a little shocked and could not bring myself to speak. Instead, I motioned him to come in, which he did briskly as though he were hoping that by moving quickly he might leave all he had said out in the hall. I shut the door behind him and immediately found my tongue. But what I then said dumbfounded me even more than what the now distraught David had said out in the hall.

"How soon can you get her here?"

~

ONLY MINUTES AFTER HE LEFT, I had to stifle an impulse to chase him down and cancel my order. I threw myself on my bed, buried my face in one of the plentiful, downy pillows, and screamed "What have I done?" over and over until I felt blood rushing from my head. When this happened, I stopped instantly. God forbid I pass out and be woken by this... this *woman*.

I leaped up and began to pace the room. I asked myself why I told him yes. I could not find an answer. I asked myself if I doubted my Love's existence. A resounding "NO!" echoed within me. I knew she was there. But then how could I think of doing something like this? Again, no answer. The next hour was spent thus: pacing, questioning in both directions, coming up with nothing, then pacing again. Every ten minutes, I would resolve to call down to David and cancel, then I would watch my hand hover just over the receiver without picking it up. What madness was this? How could I be waiting for this to happen? How could I even think of letting the diametrical opposition to all I had been searching for come into my room? But with every minute, this unknown, licentious woman came closer and closer. And I was waiting for her, and even - though I was loathed to admit it - anticipating her.

When the knock finally came, I was throwing up in the bathroom. I barely heard it as I was finishing a difficult, final heave. (The turkey sandwich and fries had not digested completely and were thus a bit clumpy coming back up.) I waited to see if my ears were deceiving me. But the light, purposeful knock came again. I stood up and looked in the mirror. What I saw wasn't pretty. I was ashen and haggard-looking. My hair was disheveled from constantly running my hands through it for the last hour and a half. Again came a knock, this time a little louder and more resolute. Oh anguish of anguish, what my restive breast felt when I finally cried out:

"Just a minute, I'll be right there!"

I could not pause. I would not wait. The time had come to face the force that had led me to this point. I hastily splashed some water on my face and straightened out my clothes and hair. I then brushed my teeth as the scent of vomit was heavy on my breath. I glanced in the mirror again. My expression resembled that of an unpopular teenage girl on receiving the news that for some as yet unexplained reason the current high school heartthrob had unexpectedly dropped by just as she was finishing a lengthy and extensive pimple-popping spree: a look which was both highly thrilled and deeply pained. Nonetheless, when I finally left the bathroom, I walked calmly to the door to meet my fate. Nothing could save me now, I thought; I must go through with whatever destiny had ordained.

When I opened the door, I was shocked by what I saw, but for a far different reason than I had expected. Standing there was, of course, a young woman. But she was nothing like I thought she would be. She wore a large-brimmed, black straw hat, a simple (yet graceful) light off-white cotton dress, a large black belt, and a pair of low-heeled, black leather shoes. Her face was not innocent or sweet, but nothing about it suggested the hardness I had expected to find in at least one feature. In fact, it was soft, almost vulnerable. Her lips were full, without being too voluptuous, and were covered with a discreet burnished red. Her cheekbones were distinct but did not achieve the arched look of a model. Her hair was a sandy blonde and hung at her shoulders, framing her oval face. And her eyes were warm — almond-shaped and a radiant green with flecks of yellow and gold near the pupils. In concert with her demeanor, which seemed relaxed and unpretentious, she came across as a lovely young woman I imagined one might meet at an early evening, upscale cocktail party.

"May I come in?" she asked in a confident but completely unassuming tone.

She smiled a slight, friendly little smile and raised her brow as she asked. I felt a strange weakness in my limbs. My heart fluttered, but in a very different way than it had before. I stood stock still gazing into her eyes. I could not move. She must have sensed this, for she reached out tentatively and took me by the hand, which I gave without protest. She then led me into my room and shut the door behind us.

Once inside, she began to lead me towards the bed. I tensed up and stopped following. She turned back to me and smiled an understanding yet playfully coaxing smile. I pulled my hand from hers, walked over to the table, and sat down in a chair. Up to this point, she had not once come across as trying to be sexual. Nor had she appeared patronizing. All her movements and expression seemed to spring from the same genuine source. Her smile and manner continued to express this as she walked over to the bed, sat down and leaned back, stretching her straightened arms behind her to rest on her hands.

"What's your name?" she asked after a few moments of observing me tranquilly.

"Spencer," I said, noting the flat, almost dead way I said it.

It was how she fielded this, I think, that made me know I was going to like her. She did not tell me it was a nice name. She did not say something stupid, like, "Oh, like *Spencer for Hire?*" She did not say she had known someone once name Spencer and that she had liked him. She made no attempt at idle chit-chat whatsoever.

"Hmm," was the only sound she made.

She then stood up, walked over to the window a few feet from me, pulled the curtain open, and stood there gazing out for several minutes without saying anything. She seemed so natural that it began to strike me as kind of peculiar, given the circumstance. But I was still taken by it. Nothing seemed forced with her. She had taken off her hat, and the last rays of the sun now shown upon her hair, the hazy yellow light giving it a soft golden hue. After a few more minutes of silence, during which the atmosphere in the room became infused with an almost somber feeling, she finally spoke.

"It's hard, isn't it, Spencer."

She said this without looking at me. It was obviously a statement, not a question. I moved not a muscle and said not a word. I just watched this strange and beautiful young woman standing near me and something stirred in me; something became alert, like a dosing sentry roused by a distant, unidentifiable, yet long anticipated noise.

"Sometimes I honestly don't think I can make it," she continued in a steady and solemn but markedly unsentimental tone. "Don't get me wrong. I don't feel sorry for myself or anything. Obviously, lots of people have it much worse than I do. It's just that sometimes it just starts to feel too heavy, like I'm going to break from the weight of it all."

Each word she spoke thawed my frozen soul. I had thought I was alive. I had believed my soul was burning with love for my Darling. But in these few moments, I realized I had felt nothing. Only now did I truly know what it was to feel. And this woman before me had made it so.

During this whole time, she had never once looked at me. But now, she turned her eyes straight to mine. Again her expression was not sentimental. It was serious. Her words resonated in her features. No smile played across her lips to undermine what she'd said. No arched brow suggested emotional subterfuge. Though I searched them for a sign, her eyes did not glitter with deception. They were steady and confirmed that she believed deeply in the things she'd said.

Where I found the strength, I do not know, but I stood up. She did not move. Her eyes had not left mine since she had turned to me. I found myself moving toward her. I felt as though I were floating, gliding over the ground toward her; but, in spite of this sensation, covering the short distance between us seemed to swallow a disproportionately large amount of time. When I finally reached her, we stood looking into each other's eyes. Then, finally, she reached up and kissed me. It was a soft, light kiss, but it lingered. It was tender. It was sweet. It was a kiss from a lover.

I could never have imagined how the act of consummation actually ended up being. Of course, I had tried to guess what it might be like. But none of my suppositions came near what it truly was. I felt we were more spiritual than physical beings. The whole process was both physical and metaphysical symbiosis. Whatever I gave, she received as though it served some preordained function. Whenever she gave, the ecstasy evoked seemed a perfect manifestation of the necessity of our union. No words passed between us. Words would have sullied it. It was a pure experience. And as I drifted off to sleep in her arms, I knew I was (at long last) where I had always been meant to be.

∼

When I woke the next morning, I did not come quickly to consciousness. In fact, it took several minutes to realize the bed was empty. But the instant I realized it, I sat bolt upright and scanned the room for any sign of my visitor. I saw nothing. I listened closely for any sounds I might have missed coming from the bathroom. All I heard was the pounding of my heart.

Bounding out of bed, I threw on some clothes and made for the door. As I ran out, I knocked a bell boy (not David, which of course pissed me off) square on his ass. I saw what looked like a note next to a silver platter on the floor. Seizing the scrap of paper without addressing the bell boy - who was now in the process of apologizing to me for having been in my way - I opened it and prepared to see a note of departure from this woman I felt certain was my Love.

I saw instead a summary of my bill. I was about to throw it to the ground and careen down the hall to find David when a certain figure on the bill jumped out at me. Next to the description "miscellaneous" was a charge for fifteen hundred dollars. My heart fell to my shoes. My face stung as though I'd been slapped. My mouth fell open and my stomach buckled. I did not have the strength to fight it. I dropped to my knees and commenced dry-heaving.

This lasted only a minute or so but was very painful. Fighting through my lightheadedness, I regained my feet and seized the bell-boy, who had been showing nervous concern by lightly, though hesitantly, patting me on the back.

"Where the fuck is David?" I hissed, as I pulled him up to me.

"I don't... I don't know," he stuttered, his face white with fear.

"What the fuck do you mean, you don't know?" I shrieked in a way that even frightened me a little as I heard its echo die down the hall.

"He's on his day off, sir. I don't know where he is because it's his day off," whimpered the now trembling bell-boy.

"Well, where does he live then? You can at least tell me that, can't you?" I demanded, reverting back to the hiss as I was worried about drawing people out into the hall.

"We're not supposed to give out the addresses of employees," he stammered. But when he saw the fury surge up in my eyes, he cowed and sputtered out, "Wait, wait, he's not at home anyway. I just remembered, he works at Disneyland on his days off."

In a flash, I reached in my pocket and threw several crumpled bills at him (they could have been ones, twenties, or hundreds for all I knew or cared) and bolted off, leaving him there quivering.

I paced to and fro, wringing my hands, barely able to contain my madness while my car was brought round. My whole life rested on getting that little son-of-a-bitch and pumping him for all he knew about my Love. When the car came around, I opened the door, grabbed the valet, and threw him to the ground. Once behind the wheel, I saw the hotel manager standing with his mouth agape next to the obviously still shaken bell-boy.

"Mr. Askew!" he roared in genuine astonishment, making me pause for a moment.

"I am sorry," he said, punctuating each word like a teacher remonstrating a pupil, "but I cannot have you treating our employees this way."

"Oh, fuck you!" I shouted with undisguised scorn. He had begun to walk towards me, but this stopped him dead and his mouth swung open again.

I slammed the accelerator to the floorboard and screeched off. Tires squealed, horns blared, and fingers flew as I shot out into traffic. I was unfazed, noting the clamor only absentmindedly. I turned west, though just why I don't know, and blazed a trail down Wilshire Blvd. slicing through the traffic like a slaloms skier carves up gates.

It took me several frenetic minutes to realize I had no idea where I was going. I pulled into a gas station and asked for directions. I was distressed but did calm down enough to make sure to get the directions right. I even bought a map (having left the other back in my room) just to be on the safe side. When I set out again, I felt relatively sure I could reach my destination - Anaheim - without too much difficulty.

To calm myself further, I drove at top speed. I knew this was foolish. I risked being pulled over, which would have been catastrophic in my state of mind. I might have said anything to get away and did not discount the idea of avoiding the former situation completely by trying to outrun any pursuing CHP or LAPD. Amazingly (when viewed in light of my driving, which was not only speedy but erratic to boot), I was unhindered by any officers of the law. In fact (and again), no one seemed even to look in my general direction.

I arrived in Anaheim within the hour and began following the signs to Disneyland, which dotted the landscape, carefully guiding all would be funseekers to their chosen destination. Once in the enormous Disneyland parking lot, I trudged along in the lot traffic, following the directions of strategically placed Disneyland employees. I also didn't mind going slowly (there were occasional stops because of traffic) because it gave me a chance to check out the parking lot employees to see if David was among them. I came to the conclusion on the drive down that my interrogation of the bell-boy had been woefully inadequate. Had I remained calmer, I might have been able to glean some useful information from him. I did not have a clue as to what capacity David worked in and, given the sheer size of this Metropolis of Fun, this was a very major oversight. As I got out of the car, I resolved to do my best to remain calm at all costs from that point forward.

It was mid-morning by this time, and the parking lot was teeming with life. Families of painfully regular folk were marching their way toward the entrance gates. The children sprung and bounced around the parents, screaming and shrieking and generally getting on my nerves. I tried to distract myself by eyeing the various Disney employees in search of David. But I did not see him. So I would have to go in the park then filling, more and more each moment, with frenzied, fun-lusting children such as those who were presently annoying me. The prospect did not thrill me, but I had no other option.

Before I entered the actual park, I inspected each ticket booth for David. Of course, he wasn't there. Since I planned to canvass the whole park to find that tip-taking bastard if necessary, I figured I'd better have full access to every ride and attraction. I bought the largest packet of tickets available and entered with the rest of the widening throng.

I got a map for orientation and began combing the park, systematically crossing off every place I did not find him. I was thorough. I even went on rides in case he was working back in the mechanisms of one of them. I rode the *Pirates of the Caribbean, The Matterhorn, Space Mountain,* even *It's a Small World* - the last nearly prompting me to strangle the child next to me, who managed somehow to sing along above the din, off-key. I went on the River Boat. I saw various shows, in Frontier Land, in Fantasy Land. I perused the arcades and games of chance. I went into all the shops and restaurants. I even went to see Lincoln "speak." Other than the fact that the latter reminded me of that skinny, scary hostess at that restaurant in San Francisco, nothing came of it. I hadn't even seen anyone who resembled him.

I was thinking of slipping behind the scenes when it occurred to me that he might be one of the various roaming cartoon characters. I felt a little stupid for not having considered this before. But I gave myself a break. I had been under a lot of pressure and could not expect myself to think of every possibility. Besides, after watching them for a bit, I saw how I managed to ignore them. Strange though it may seem, they blended so much with the surreal landscape it was not hard to just not see them. Or at least I consoled myself that this was the case.

I started to study the various characters I stumbled across. I searched for any characteristic that might betray what I had seen so far of David's manner. But trying to distinguish any one character from another proved difficult since they all acted pretty much the same. All would bend down and pat children on the head in essentially the same way. They all posed for pictures in a similar mode. I started to think he might be Donald Duck. This character seemed to be the most plucky of the ones I'd seen, and David had always had a spunky air about him. After a while, I went up and stood right in front of him. When I looked straight into his beak and got no unique response, I concluded it wasn't him. I felt I would know him by some unconscious gesture of recognition on his part. But this guy just went through the standard motions. Then he ignored me.

I was about to give up when Goofy came round the corner on Main St. I don't know what it was, but something about him struck me. He had a gaggle of children at his feet with whom he was playing the clown. The more I watched him, the more I felt sure it was David. I had seen him play with one little kid in the lobby the day before while I was having one of many drinks and his movements were almost exactly like this Goofy's. Still, I hung back a little while longer just to make sure.

When I finally went up to him, I just acted like I didn't want anything but to be like everyone else hanging around Goofy. The dead giveaway to me that I had my man was when he singled me out by waving at me, then coming up and patting me on the head. After he showed his hand like that, I was having none of it.

"All right, David," I said firmly. "I want to know who she was, her name, who she worked for, everything. And I want to know it right now."

At this, he cocked his head, then reached up and scratched it as if in confusion. But I was not going to be thrown by amateur theatrics.

"I'm serious, man," I said firmly into his big nose, leaving no doubt that he could hear me, but without raising my voice. "I want to know everything you know about her, David. You'd better tell me right now."

To this last demand he just shrugged his shoulders, spread out his arms with his palms up, pretending he did not know or even understand what I was talking about. This infuriated me, but I did my best to master my anger. This was the only person I knew with any connection to my Darling; I had to try to control myself while remaining persistent. He had started to amble away, but I just trotted along next to him and kept repeating my demand. When he stopped to play with the children fumbling around his feet, I was in his face. He seemed determined to ignore me, but I was just as determined that he address me. Finally, he stopped in his big floppy tracks and repeated the shrugging gesture. This time, however, he managed somehow to convey a genuine exasperation with me. And I, at last, could contain my anger and resentment no longer.

"You miserable son-of-a-bitch," I howled right up his nose. "I've given you probably two thousand dollars in tips, and you won't even answer me! All right then! If you won't talk to me, then you'll never talk to anyone again. I'll rip your mother fucking tongue out of your head!"

With a bloodcurdling scream, I leaped on him and sent both of us tumbling to the ground. I heard children shrieking as I clutched his neck and wrung it with all my might. Gasping and choking came from inside the suit. After a few moments of struggle, he managed to get a hold on my arms and succeeded in pulling them from his neck. The deftness of this maneuver caught me off guard, and before I knew it, he had flipped me on my back and was punching me solidly in the face with his padded Goofy gloves.

"I'll show you who the son-of-a-bitch is you piece of shit," I heard a voice which sounded not at all like what I'd expected.

"David?" I shouted out as I fended off his blows. "Is that you?"

"I'm not David, you stupid bastard," I heard this deeper, much more resonant voice than I knew David's to be, bawl out from behind the mask. "I tried to make you see that, you god damned idiot, but you just wouldn't get the picture!"

He had stopped hitting me to yell this. The children around us had never ceased shrieking and a crowd had begun to gather. It would be only a matter of minutes before a resident Disneyland swat team descended upon the situation. During my travels around the park, I had observed the good-natured, Orwellian efficiency with which it was operated. Thus I was sure some crack security squad was certainly *en route* to nab me.

But I was not about to be caught so easily. With every ounce of strength I had, I flung myself up and knocked Goofy over on his back again. I scrambled to my feet and stood for a moment like a cornered wildcat with the crowd around me. Taking cue from this break, the children rushed to my adversary's aid. I saw people scowling and heard them cussing me. Some even made as though they were going to grab me, but I snarled and plunged into them before they had the chance. Cutting a swath through them, I broke out from the crowd's edge and raced off into Fantasyland to lose anyone who might try to follow.

After hiding in some bushes for around an hour, I saw the afternoon light was starting to fade. I figured enough time had probably passed to make it safe for me to venture out and hopefully leave the park unobserved. I acted as casual as possible to keep attention from myself. When I walked right down Main St., nobody gave me a second glance. Well, actually, one red-haired, pig-tailed girl around ten years old did stare at me while crinkling her brow as if confused by something. But she said nothing, and I was very near an exit, so I just turned away and ran out to the parking lot.

FINDING THE BEAUTY was more of a trial than I thought it would be. By the time I got to it, dusk was settling. I got in, put on a pair of sunglasses to disguise myself, and joined the line of cars slowly moving toward the parking lot exit. I was deeply depressed that I had not found David. Without him, I had no idea how to find her. Was it possible that my Darling had been given to me for only this short time? But that was impossible! We were meant to be together forever, not just one night.

For some reason, I recalled the "miscellaneous" charge just then and shuddered. No. It could not have gone to her, I thought. She must have been tricked somehow. She could not have gone that far down simply because I had not yet arrived in her life. I could not believe that. I would not believe that! Desperate she might have become, but not that desperate. Still, I was having difficulty uncovering what motive could have gotten her to my room. I was pondering this to no avail when I reached an exit.

I noticed a small crowd of people standing very near this exit. They were apparently watching some protester. I saw a single picket sign bobbing up and down above their heads, but I couldn't quite make out what it said in the dim dusk light. I cannot say why, but for some reason, I wanted to read it. So instead of following the car in front of me out to the road, I pulled over near the crowd to get a better look. From this closer vantage point, I was finally able to read it.

Painted on one side in large red letters was "Life is not a dream;" on the other side, painted the same way, was "Hope does not lie in lies." I could make no sense of this, yet it intrigued me nonetheless. When I turned the engine off and rolled down the windows, I immediately heard a woman's voice chanting above the rush of the cars going by. I could not have said just what, but there was something familiar about the voice. I listened more closely and made out the words:

"Evil exists, don't deny it! If you sell only good, we won't buy it!"

I could not imagine what this woman was trying to accomplish with all this, but the whole idea of it, coupled with the familiar tenor of her voice, piqued me enough to make me want to have a look at her. I rolled the windows back up, got out, and locked the Beauty; then I stationed myself in a spot which gave me a clear line of sight when she marched passed.

I saw a beautiful young woman dressed exactly like the evil queen from *Snow White*: she wore the same long, tight-fitting black and purple gown, which covered her arms and head. And there was, of course, her crown of gold. She had also made her face up to look the part. I felt a shiver run through me when I got my first clear view of her face, but could not have said particularly why I felt this. The sun was setting, but it was not at all cold. Just then, someone from the crowd, which had been almost completely quiet, spoke out and distracted me.

"Hey, what are you trying to prove anyway?" a man called

out sarcastically. "Disney puts evil in its movies. There's always a villain. Look at who you're supposed to be."

"And the villains always lose, don't they?" shot back the young woman. "Good always triumphs in Disney, but that's not how it is in life. Evil has won, is winning, and will always win."

Her tone was calm and even, and she spoke loud enough to be heard, but not at all as one might have expected after hearing her before. There was a noble quality to the way she spoke, though there was a subtle condescension — maybe even a tremor of contempt — to it. It was just as if she actually *were* a queen addressing a subject who had been impertinent enough to question her. Apparently, she impressed her audience; no one else spoke. She then walked around silently and surveyed the crowd superciliously. When she passed in front of me, I saw her steady, dark, mesmerizing eyes and felt a surge of energy course through me. Traffic was still racing by, but I heard her unwavering, poised voice clearly when she spoke again.

"Do we actually need to cite the examples of what we are speaking of? All right then... one example from history, just one, banal though its evocation has become, might show you..."

She paused, surveyed the crowd, then said slowly, "The Holocaust."

"But we beat the Nazis!" someone shouted from the crowd after a tense minute.

"Did we bring the six million Jews they murdered back to life?" she smoothly replied without missing a beat.

No one said a word. When she arched her brow and smiled

a slight, scornful smile while she studied the crowd, I was able to look more closely at her face. As I have said, her voice had seemed familiar from the beginning. Now I saw something familiar in her looks as well. The make-up had thrown me at first, but I could see - I felt absolutely sure, though I could still barely believe it - that this was the very same woman who had visited me the night before. I looked again, more closely, just to be sure. Except for the eye color, she was exactly the same. I nearly fainted in rapture. I wanted to scream with joy and was very near to doing so when a Disneyland security guard, flanked by two Anaheim police officers, jostled me on their way to apprehend my Darling.

∼

I WAITED ALL NIGHT LONG in my car across the street from the Anaheim police station. When I first arrived, I went in to find out when they were going to release her. But, since I could prove no relationship, they would tell me nothing. So I had to content myself with waiting.

In the end, my Love had been a tad too resistant. All the security guard and police had wanted was that she get off Disney property. She had remained calm but was firmly against the proposal. Then, in an apparently irrational move, she had slapped one of the police officers. This was not taken well. In a flash, my Love was cuffed, scuttled over to a nearby patrol car, and whisked away. It happened so fast that she was in the back of the squad car before I could decide whether or not to come to her rescue.

Of course, I felt awful. My equivocation had cost my Darling her freedom. I was worried sick that she might never forgive me if I told her what I had (or rather had not) done. She might think I had been too afraid to risk getting thrown into jail for her. I cursed myself for being so indecisive. Here I had traveled all this way, enduring all sorts of hardships in order to find her, and all she might see was that I had been incapable of helping her when she needed it most.

I was still fretting about this when she emerged from the police station. She was in the same Evil Queen garb, but her make-up was gone. In the early morning light, I felt more certain than before that this woman and the one who had made love to me were one and the same. Again, for some inexplicable reason, I could not bring myself to approach her. It wasn't exactly fear, only something in me that was uncertain. She walked out to the curb and stood there only a matter of moments before a cab came and picked her up. I turned my car around and followed her at a distance that ensured I would not lose her, but one that would also not allow me to be easily observed.

"Oh, slake my thirst, Love," I said to the back of her head in the cab window, as if she might somehow hear me and turn around. "Look at me. Look at me! I'm dying of thirst for you. Turn and help me, Love!"

But she did not turn around. As the taxi shot down the freeways for the next forty-five minutes, her head seemed locked in the straight forward position. At various intervals, I considered pulling up next to her to try to get her attention. But I always talked myself out of it. With an LA cab driver at the wheel, she was too potentially elusive. A word from her, and he could lose me in a snap. So I abandoned all ideas of confrontation and contented myself with following.

Eventually, we reached a bland-looking apartment complex in an area that was not so nice as I expected my Dear would choose to live. I parked down the block, and I watched her pay the fare, then walk up to an apartment on the second floor. Again, I was torn by indecision. I could not decide whether or not to go up and make my declaration of love. It seemed absurd that she was so close, but that I would not go to her. Finally, I decided the moment was not right. I felt it inside. I also felt I would know, just as I had always known before, when the right time was to make my move.

There was another thing as well. During the last day and a half, I had stayed awake thinking of what had happened between us in my hotel room. I was bewildered by my Darling's behavior. I could not find a way to reconcile the fifteen hundred dollar charge in my mind. And no amount of rationalization was helping. The fact was that there was no way she could have known it was me who was waiting for her. But I was in deep anguish over the idea that she could behave in such a way without knowing it was me. Even I, disposed as I was to give her the benefit of the doubt, could draw really only one conclusion.

But oh, the agony of that conclusion! If she was acting this way on a regular basis, she could not help but be lost to me. Her soul would invariably be corrupted beyond repair. I felt a creeping, ominous dread at this idea. My body ached and trembled to think of her going from man to man, devoid of emotions, using her body while forgetting the treasure that it housed. My treasure! What level of degeneration must she have reached to do this? Was I too late? The evidence made my soul quake in fear.

After mulling this over for several hours (during which time my Darling was napping, I'm sure) she finally emerged from her apartment. She had transformed, yet again. At first, I wondered if she had a similar-looking roommate. But I studied her more closely and soon discovered my Love. She wore a plain white T-shirt, a pair of faded blue jeans, and caramel-colored hiking boots. Her hair was tied back in a loose bun, wisps falling around her face. It appeared darker than when she had come to my suite. She also wore a pair of rimless glasses and had a light brown leather backpack thrown over her shoulder.

I decided to follow her on foot as I felt that would be less conspicuous. When she was about half a block away, I got out of my car and began tailing her. She walked at a relatively quick pace, and I felt a bit lightheaded trying to keep up. I realized not sleeping or eating for the last two days had been a mistake. But what else could I have done? I could not have risked losing her again. Sleeping and eating were luxuries I simply could not afford.

It wasn't long before we reached the USC campus, which she continued onto. I must admit I was surprised. I had not expected my Darling to still be a student. She looked around my age. But then I thought she might be doing some sort of graduate study. The idea that she was focused on something like this sent a flood of hope through me. It might mean she had not abandoned herself completely to a life of decadence. But my fears of irreparable damage to herself were not totally dispelled.

I followed her into a building but stayed out in the hall when she followed a group of students, whom I noticed were carrying psychology books, into a classroom. People were giving me strange looks as they walked by, I assume because of my appearance. My clothes were rumpled, and I hadn't shaved or washed up in general for around two days. I started to get a little nervous about this. I was afraid I might be taken for a street person and hauled away for loitering. But in spite of my mounting anxiety about m state, I stayed where I was. I could not risk ducking into a bathroom to clean myself up, even for a moment. If I lost her again after struggling so long and hard to find her, it might unhinge me completely.

Around an hour later, the class let out. I started to panic when she did not exit with the rest of her classmates. I waited only a minute or two longer, then went up to the door to see if she was still in the class or had left by another door. I was calmed when I saw her talking to an older woman who was obviously the professor. When I saw my Love gathering her books, I high-tailed it down the hall and hid myself in an alcove full of various vending machines.

Here I saw a chance to pick up a little energy and possibly arrest the now almost constant dizziness I felt, as well as the wrenching pain in my stomach. I bought a few candy bars, some potato chips, and a Pepsi; then crammed it in, chomped it up, and washed it all down in record time. I kept poking my head out every few seconds to make sure my Love hadn't come out of the classroom. When I'd finished my makeshift repast, I peeked out just in time to see her rounding the corner at the other end of the hall.

I bolted after her, nearly running into several people walking along in the hall. I careened around the corner and nearly ran into my Darling, who had stopped apparently to read some announcements on a bulletin board. Had there been a wall rather than a men's bathroom door right there, I would have made a wreck of myself. I saw with my peripheral vision that I had startled my Dear, because she turned toward me abruptly when I went by. Fortunately, no one was coming out of the bathroom, so I slammed through the door and stopped myself on the bathroom sink.

A quick look in the mirror betrayed that not only my clothes looked terrible. My face was pale, my eyes were bloodshot, and my hair was a mess as well. Losing no time, for fear of missing my Love, I hastily splashed some water on my face and tried to straighten my hair and clothes. Within a minute, I made myself look at least a bit more presentable. But the nervous, pained expression on my face, I could not remove. I knew that would be up to her.

I stuck my head out the door and panicked again when I saw she was not there. Darting out the nearest door, I scanned the courtyard and, to my great relief, spotted her almost immediately. Trying to assume a casual, evening stroll kind of air, I followed her. Once or twice I broke into a sprint when I felt she was putting too much distance between us. Finally, she went into another building. Again, I followed her.

The building turned out to be a theater. I was not surprised that my Darling might be an aspiring actress. The performance outside of Disneyland alone showed her thoroughly capable of it. She had carried that off with style and ease, handling the crowd like a seasoned veteran. Her manner, combined with her striking, unique looks, made her a natural for the stage or screen.

I thought initially about going in to watch what I assumed would be a rehearsal. I saw by a poster in the lobby that *Othello* was opening in a few weeks. My Love would, of course, make a wonderful Desdemona. I thought of her lying on that bed asleep, the jealousy-obsessed Othello hovering over her, falsely accusing her. The thought of this scene kept me from going in. They might be rehearsing it when I came in, and I decided I was in too unstable a state of mind to watch my Darling being murdered, even if I knew it was not real. I waited instead on a bench outside near the door. Within the hour, out came my Dear.

I had chosen a place that would allow me to see her, but would not be conspicuous. As a result, she appeared not to notice me when I trailed along after her. I still had not found the will to confront her. I was trying to think of the most effective way to approach her, but nothing presented itself. Suddenly, however, it appeared my Darling was going to take the bull by the horns. She stopped abruptly, turned around and marched straight at me. Stunned to a standstill, I could only wait. I considered running away, but she was too near. My thoughts were in riot. I wanted to tell her everything, but I was so distraught I knew I could never articulate what I felt.

But instead of talking to me (or even noticing me), she just walked right by. Something finally snapped in me. The moment had come. I felt fear, and yet I could stop myself no longer. She had gone only ten feet or so when I turned and called out to her.

"Stop."

I did not say it loudly, but I said it firmly and resolutely to leave no doubt that she heard me. But she didn't stop. After she walked another ten feet or so, something surged in me, and this time the word came like a shot from a cannon:

"Stop!"

To my complete surprise, she halted, as if she realized her next step would send her off a cliff. Then she turned and looked at me searchingly.

"Do I know you?" she asked.

"Yes," I said, my voice trembling from the strain.

She studied me a moment, her expression tottering between annoyance and confusion. I took several steps toward her, slowly, cautiously, as though I were approaching an only partially tamed animal.

"I'm sorry," she said in a puzzled tone. "I don't know where I know you from."

This cut me deeply, and I winced. She saw this reaction but appeared only to be further confused by it.

"I saw you at Disneyland," I said with effort. "I followed you from there."

She seemed to tense up as though unpleasantly surprised. This made me even more tense in turn. I did not want to frighten her away.

"You're... you're amazing," I stammered out.

"Yeah, well, I guess you must think so if you've been following me since the day before yesterday," she said in a cocky tone, which caught me off guard.

She walked back towards me, then stopped several feet away.

"Well, who do you work for? What do you want?"

I stared in her eyes, which she was squinting slightly in question. I felt weak in her presence. I was struggling to tip the cauldron of words boiling up in my heart.

"You," I finally said.

"Well, I'm pretty busy right now," she said matter-of-factly after looking me up and down.

"Are you with Paramount? You look really familiar to me. I've interned over there. Do you work on that lot?"

Obviously, she thought I was somebody other than who I was, and this pained me further because this was the second time we had met. How could she not feel the love we shared?

"I want you," I said, my voice breaking with the strain.

"Yeah, that part I got, but I still need to know what it is you want me for," she said, then quickly glanced at her watch. "I'm directing this play, going to school full time, and I've got other commitments as well, so I need to have an idea of what we're talking about."

The gulf of misunderstanding, as well as her impatience, appeared to be growing all the wider, and I knew I needed to define the situation as quickly as possible or risk losing her. I mustered all my courage, took several steps toward her 'til we were within arms length, and said the only thing I could think of to make her recognize me.

"It's me," I said softly, a tremor in my voice. "It's Spencer."

She continued to look puzzled. Then, slowly, a wave of recognition passed over her face. I studied her expression for anything that might betray how she was feeling. But it was difficult to read. Except for appearing to tense up again, her features - though as lovely as ever - were inscrutable. Though it was a cool day, I felt my forehead dampening. I began to tremble more than before. I even feared, as she stood there studying me, that I might lose control of my bowels. Fortunately, her face relaxed slightly and sent a flood of relief through me.

"How did you find me?" she finally asked evenly.

"I was led to you," I said, steadying my voice as much as I could.

"What do you mean?" she said, watching me suspiciously. "Who led you to me?"

"Darling, our love led me to you," I said plaintively while managing to straighten myself up and maintain our unbroken eye contact.

She breathed in deeply, then let out a sigh. I took this initially as a sigh of relief: she could breathe easy now, I had finally come. I almost reached out to take her in my arms. But in another moment, to my deep despair, I saw an expression which mingled exasperation and irritation. She then appeared to gather herself up for something, and I was afraid to hear her words.

"Look," she said. "I don't know what you want from me. I came over and gave you what you paid for. Was there a problem with the way I did it or something?"

She stood before me, incomprehensible, unfathomable. I heard her words, but I could not understand them.

"I love you," I said. "I've been searching for you, and now I found you. I'm here to save you from the life you've been leading and give you the love that you've always wanted."

She stared at me blankly. Then she looked down and her expression changed. She seemed to be considering something. Hope grew in my heart as I watched her. She began walking away. She said nothing to encourage me, but I followed anyway. After a minute or so, she began to speak.

"Okay, Spencer. Let's just say that I could love you," she said. "I mean, I do actually find you physically attractive."

Though these words should have sent a thrill through me, they did not. The matter of fact tone she was using inspired hope in nothing.

"But I could love anyone," she went on. "Anyone who fits my combined neurotic and physiological ideal. I mean, it's really completely arbitrary. We are all just the tools of our biological and neurotic processes. Look around, Spencer. Marriage is a joke today. And that's because no one is ever true to anybody but themselves. If they want to fuck someone, then they'll fuck them. It just doesn't make any difference. That's why everyone is so fucked up, and it's also why I am not and never will be in a relationship that doesn't suit my purposes.

"I've got *my* life and *my* goals. And I don't need anyone getting in my way. You or any man can have my body if it can help me get what I want. But as far as I'm concerned, my soul - if there even is such a thing - is my own to do with what I please."

These words shocked and appalled me. I stopped in my tracks. She kept walking.

"But no!" I cried, running to catch up with her. When I reached her, she did not look at me, which began to anger me.

"I'm here so that you don't have to resign yourself to that hopeless existence. If you'll just stop and look at me, you will see the truth of what I'm saying in my eyes."

She stopped abruptly and looked me in the eye, a sardonic smirk on her face. The change of expression I expected to witness never happened. She just looked me up and down, turned and began walking off in the same direction at a brisk pace.

"Look, I don't know who the hell you are, but I do know you are one fucked up customer," she said when I caught her. "I don't want any person in my life right now, let alone someone as freaked out as you. You obviously need some major help, so why don't you go and get it and leave me alone. You're starting to annoy me."

At this last sentence, the slow anger I had been feeling engorged me, and I felt something I had never anticipated feeling in the presence of my Love: rage. I knew she would be resistant, but I never imagined she could be this obstinate when actually confronted by me, her one and only Love. And even though I was not the violent kind, I felt compelled to seize her so that I might shake some sense into her. In fact, the urge was so strong I could not resist it.

I thrust my hand out and grabbed hold of her right shoulder. She stopped, appearing to give in to the force of my hand, which surprised me a little and made me think I might have a chance of prevailing with her after all. But her next maneuver laid such speculation to rest. She turned, placed her right hand on my left shoulder to steady herself, then made a quick, deft thrust with her right knee into my groin.

As can be imagined, my reaction was immediate and typical. I gasped and fell to the ground grasping the offended organ in hopes of somehow assuaging the throbbing pain already pulsating from there. I clenched my teeth and eyelids as I endured the waves of acute, aching nausea in the fetal position while rocking my body slightly. After letting a few low groans escape my lips, I opened my eyes and saw her standing, legs apart, arms akimbo, towering over me. Her expression was one of contempt. When she saw my eyes open, she leaned down close to my ear and spoke in a harsh, punctuated whisper.

"You just made a very big mistake," she said slowly and deliberately, as a teacher gives instructions to a dense student. "What I just did to you is only a sample of what I'm capable of doing to anyone who fucks with me."

She stood up and looked down at me again. With the way the sunlight fell on her face and the look in her eyes, she seemed the picture of evil to me. A chill ran through me. Though the pain had subsided almost completely, I remained in the fetal position staring up at her. After several more moments, she spoke again.

"You need to know something, Spencer: I carry a gun. I know how to use it. And I will use it if I'm pushed."

She stated this as though she were taking a vow, and I did not doubt her conviction.

I lay there in the sun after she walked away, feeling nothing. My mind was blank. I stood up slowly, unmindful of the people staring at me from safe distances. I stood there for several minutes, gazing without focus up at the sky. All at once, I started to walk. Then I began to trot. Finally, I broke into a run. I ran without aim until I came to a building. I went through a door and down a hall and through another door.

I rushed to a handicapped stall at the furthest end of the cavernous bathroom and slammed the door shut. Gripping the cool porcelain bowl at its base, I began to retch up chocolate-Pepsi flavored gruel, then bile mixed with blood. It was painful and laborious, and I thought it would never stop. When at last I did finish, I lay on the floor next to the bowl covered in sweat, but relieved for the moment. I stayed thus for I cannot say how long; it could have been an hour or only five minutes. My only gauge was the spinning ceiling, for which I waited to slow to a reasonable revolution. When it had very nearly stopped, I rolled over, put my back to the stall divider, and inched up to a sitting position. From here, I was afforded a view of the graffiti-covered wall against which this end stall butted up.

I was amazed by the plenitude of self-expression that had found its way onto this bathroom wall. As high up as a senior basketball star could reach, pornographic drawings, gang insignias, epigrams, anecdotes, philosophic blurbs, and indecipherable scrawls of every sort confronted me. I began to read them to pass the time until I gained the strength to stand up and leave. My initial amazement acquired both breadth and depth. Arguments on myriad social issues were laid out before me; inaugural statements were answered with fiery retorts, which were, in turn, responded to, sometimes by the original author, sometimes by another who wanted to join the fray. The villainy of the government seemed the topic of choice. The diatribes on this subject were uniform in their agreement that the leaders of our nation, the chief executive in particular, were incarnations of evil. I read them from top to bottom until I reached one which lay beneath them all:

"Whoever said 'the 90s will make the 60s look like the 50s' should have said, 'the 90s will make the 50s look like the 60s.' Our generation is just a bunch of scared, worthless drunks who

can't even get off their asses when the fate of the world is at stake. I'm ashamed to be young."

I read this one and began to laugh. I laughed and laughed 'til I thought I was going to be sick again.

After I calmed down a bit, I started to think it time to reassess my situation. Maybe hope had not abandoned me. I thought of my destiny, my fate. I felt it hovering above me, importuning me not to let her threat and general attitude put me off. I knew where my Darling lived, and I loved her. I tried to imagine it was only a question of thinking about what to do next. But oh, I was wounded and worn! This final episode — my Darling's spiteful words and flat denial of me as her savior — had hacked away at my recently bandaged belief, fracturing the bone, leaving me hanging from the bloody, sinuous muscle of faith.

I had, however, been battered so brutally into belief that I was afraid to let go of my faith again for fear of more punishment. So I tried to take cautious mental steps toward revising my plan to bring my Darling over to me. But I was too weak. My thoughts were insurmountably difficult to organize. My mind wandered, as did my eyes. That was when I saw it. At the top of everything on the wall (how could I have not seen it before?) scrawled in bright lipstick red was a message that finally severed the tissue which so tenuously held me up:

"You'll Die, Dreams Unrealized"

The blood rushed from my face. My heart throbbed in my ears. My mind twisted and wrenched in a convulsive fit. The room began to spin again and my stomach heaved as I lunged for the commode. My intestines felt as though they were coming up as I saw blood, pure luscious red blood, spew out of my mouth. After the initial heave, I burst out from the stall and ran mad out onto the campus, out to the hopeful light of the sun.

But there was no sun. Clouds of black sulfurous smoke billowed up to the sky, blocking its light. Sharp cracks of gunfire stabbed into frantic, wailing sirens. Quick, harsh shouts mixed with short, piercing screams. Helicopters approached, incrementally adding to the furor, finally swallowing all other sounds as they passed above.

And none of this stopped me. My eyes stung. My ears ached. My brain was seared and throbbed with pain. My whole body cried out, begged me to lay it down. But I would not. I could not. All I heard and saw seemed right. I welcomed it. I was pulled to it. Into the streets, into the roar and the fire. Hell had opened its doors, and I ran to my annihilation as hard and as fast I could.

∼

I COULD NOT TELL YOU HOW I HAD GOTTEN THERE. I did not know how much time had passed or where I had been during that time. I just knew that I was on an empty residential street, somewhere, soaked in sweat, bile, and blood and breathing hard. My head was still spinning, and there was a loud buzzing coming from somewhere. I was trying to scream loud enough to make it stop or at least drown it out. My hands over my ears and my eyes bulging open; my pose was like that of people in science fiction movies when confronted with a sound and a sight they find unbearable. So hard was I focused on that sound that I barely saw the huge, white car careening around the corner. But when I realized it was headed straight for me, it received the whole of my attention.

This laser-like focus did nothing for me, however. I did not have time to think, let alone jump out of the way. I heard the motor revving. I saw the driver — a young black man — bearing down on me. I dropped my hands to my side and closed my eyes. Everything in my body became calm. I felt at peace with this certain, mindless death. Then, at the last possible moment, the car veered to the right. The wind the car created as it passed seemed to spin me around, and I saw another young black man brandishing a Schlitz Malt Liquor can as he hung out the passenger window and yelled, "Haaah haaaaah, whittiiee!" Whether they turned right or left, I could not have said. I only had time to see a small brown Toyota pick-up truck rolling to a stop in front of me from the other direction before I crumpled to the pavement and lost my tenuous hold on consciousness.

My memories from this point become very spotty. The next thing I vaguely recall is the sounds of a tense discussion between two women taking place somewhere above me. Then my eyes rolled open to see the dirty roof of a camper shell. I closed them and felt below me the hum of tires rolling at a high speed over the pavement. Next, I was flailing around and screaming at two round, brown faces which stared at me in awe and dismay from the other side of a window in the camper shell. Again, darkness.

Then I was somewhere else. There were no tires humming, and I saw again a round face, only one this time, reflecting flickering candlelight and floating over me like a moon keeping the darkness at bay. I forced my eyes to stay open, but they seemed to be coated with a thin layer of Vaseline. I could not distinguish any features on the face, though I sensed something tender in it. Then I felt hot and heard a voice (possibly - indeed very likely - mine) starting out soft and thin, then building to an eerie howl. Next, I heard a woman shout, then felt an authoritative slap on my face and the screaming stopped, and I felt cold, then hot again. I heard someone weeping (me again, I'm pretty sure), then I felt a cool hand on my forehead and opened my eyes to see a more oblong-shaped face just above me. Next, I was being rocked in someone's arms, and the light became thin, then all was black.

Whispers drifted into my ear, coaxing me awake. I was warm, but comfortably so this time. My head was buried in soft, fluffy pillows, and my naked body was ensconced in smooth, clean linens. My eyes rolled sluggishly open. A dusky, reddish light, as if it were passing through a thick membrane, suffused the small room in which I was situated. Again I could distinguish almost nothing around me. But I kept my eyes opened, and the light grew stronger and brighter. I was eventually able to make out the edges of my bed, which I then followed up to a figure hovering just above its end.

With great concentration I was able to discern a long-haired Christ framed in gold staring down on me from black-velvet. After a bit longer, I saw he was, as would be expected, regarding me with infinitely forgiving and merciful eyes. I blinked several times, then stared back in his eyes. They remained dark, mesmerizing pools for several minutes until I was able to distinguish the black pupils from the irises of blue. In spite of myself, in my weakened state I could not help feeling some comfort from those eyes.

During the whole of this focusing exercise, the whispery, undulating buzz of an oscillating fan continued, intermittently sending a soft rush of cool air over my face. Mentally I began to follow the path my eyes had taken, attempting to make certain abstract distinctions. I observed first that the noise of this fan was different from the noise that had lured me back to consciousness. Somehow I was sure it was voices I had heard. No sooner had I thought this than I heard these whispering voices again. I looked over to the door behind which they seemed to be coming. The voices stopped abruptly. This made me anxious. Was I perhaps being watched? Had the occupants of that truck, which I could only vaguely recollect, decided to deposit me in the nearest mental hospital? Given what I could recall of my behavior, I could not have blamed them.

I quickly allayed my fears, however, by glancing around the room. Nothing institutional about it. A chest of drawers painted white stood below Christ at the foot of the bed; a small desk, also white, with a lamp on it and an accompanying chair over by the window; a nightstand (white again) with a lamp on it as well next to the bed; plus a bookstand filled with worn-looking paperbacks.

Just then, I saw the door opening slowly. Though my weakened state kept me from becoming overly excited, still, I was uncertain. If I wasn't in an institution, just where was I? And who had been taking care of me for however long I had been in this semi-conscious, hallucinogenic state? The last question was partly answered by a broad, calico-covered back making its way around the door. A round-faced old Hispanic woman turned around and placed a tray with a steaming bowl on the desk. She turned toward me, took two steps in my direction, then stood still when she saw I was looking at her. For the moment, we just exchanged stares.

"Hola," she said. She smiled nervously while looking about coyly as if she were a schoolgirl. I managed a smile back, which seemed to put her at ease. She regarded me, her hands cupping her elbows and her eyes calm and maternal. I found her gaze soothing.

But after a minute or so like this, a door slammed from somewhere outside the room, causing both the old woman and me to jump. Her expression became nervous again, and she hurriedly left the room. I was trying to piece together how it was that I had come to this room in the house with this old Hispanic woman when in walked another woman. I could not see her well, but something about her made me think she was much younger than the other. She seemed more purposeful than the older woman. As soon as she came into the room, I had a strange feeling about her that produced a flutter somewhere in my gut.

"So," I heard her say in a Hispanic accent, one that was not pronounced, yet still had an edge to it, "you've finally decided to quit this laying around and sleeping all the time, eh?"

She stepped boldly over to the window and opened the blinds with a single clattering stroke. The sharp light from the mid-morning sun spewed into the room, forcing my eyes shut. I felt her sit on the bed next to my knees. She grabbed my right leg and shook it firmly.

"Come on, you silly thing, open up your eyes and see who's been taking care of your lazy self for the last two weeks."

Slowly, I did as she said. It took them a full minute to adjust to the light, but my eyes finally came into focus. I saw before me a Hispanic woman in her mid-thirties. She had long, wavy black hair. Her face was oblong and her cheeks hung down, threatening to fold into full-blown jowls. Her nose was long, narrow at the top, flaring out into a bulb at the tip, strikingly like that of a proboscis monkey. Her dark eyes were a contradiction: both languid and alert. Her lips were full and her mouth was wide and was presently smiling, or rather smirking. My timid, tepid brain was still somewhat dazed, but I had begun to wonder about who she was when she spoke again.

"Before you get started pestering me with a bunch of questions about where you are and how you got to this place to be abused by this funny-looking Panamanian woman, sit still, and I'll tell you the basic story while I feed you your lunch."

She then began to situate me. First, she pulled me up and leaned me forward, then put some pillows up behind me. She laid me back with an odd sort of gentle-firmness. Then she got up, brought the tray from the desk over, set it on my lap, sat on the bed next to me again, and began feeding me the soup. I could hardly keep all the questions I had brimming up inside me from spilling out. I was also anticipating what she was going to say, however, so I followed her directions and stayed quiet.

"Mama and Aunt Juanitá brought you here," she began as she ladled the soup into my mouth. "They were coming home from their weekly visit to Costco across town when all that craziness broke out on the streets. It was madness, I tell you. I was watching on the TV, and the helicopters were shooting their cameras down on it, showing it all. There were buildings burning and people breaking into shops all because they were mad about some Rodney King getting put in jail or not getting out of jail or something. It was all right there on TV, but it was real. And I knew it was real because I heard people screaming and running around and then gunshots and sirens, so I knew something big was happening. Even though I was worried sick about Mama and Aunt Juanitá, I stayed inside and waited. I knew they could take care of themselves and that, if I went out, I would probably just get sucked up into all that mess and get carried away and then they'd come home to an empty house and worry and wonder about what happened to me. Hey, pay attention, stupid! Don't get this bedspread dirty or I'll make you clean it yourself."

Here she stopped and scowled at me while roughly wiping with a paper towel some soup I'd let dribble onto my chin. I had already gotten so engrossed in the story that I'd forgotten all about eating. I mumbled an apology, and she continued.

"Anyway, like I said, Mama and Aunt Juanitá were in the middle of all this stuff I'm telling you about. They were afraid to go home the regular way because they heard on the radio about all that was going on in that direction. So they decided to take some back roads. That was where they picked you up from the middle of the street. They said you were all bloody and passed out. The passed out part I have a hard time believing the way you were raving when you got here. I guess at first they argued about what to do, whether to just leave you there or to take you home. Aunt Juanitá, she's more like me, practical, so she said they ought to drag you up to someone else's doorstep and then just get home. But Mama — she's always been softer — she says that they should take you home because there was no telling what someone might do to a white boy like you laying out there like that all unconscious. I guess they argued pretty hard about it, but, obviously, Mama finally won, and they loaded you up and brought you here. I told them they were crazy and asked them why they did it, but they started arguing again so much that I finally just told them to both shut up. I'm warning you, if you don't start paying attention, you won't get any more soup!"

She actually yelled this time and had such a mean look on her face that she really did scare me. I must have looked pretty sheepish because her expression softened after a moment (I think she even smiled a little), then she daubed the dribble off my chin much more tenderly than the time before.

"Well, I thought at first that maybe we should try to take you to the hospital," she said, continuing to feed me as she talked. "This is what Aunt Juanitá was lobbying for pretty strong. You looked so beat up, you smelled and had blood all over you and were acting so crazy, she thought you might be dangerous or something. I looked at you, and I knew I could handle you no problem, but then you were saying such weird things, and there was that blood which worried me, so I thought maybe Aunt Juanitá might be right. But Mama said that because of all the wild things going on in the street, it was probably a bad idea to try to get to the hospital and that the hospital was probably full of all sorts of people right now anyway, and that she liked the look of your face on top of everything and that we could probably take care of you just fine. Well, she definitely had a point about how things were outside. We could see on TV that it wasn't getting any calmer. I said that we could keep you for the night and then just see about taking you to the hospital the next day.

"But the next day, we saw on TV and heard outside that it wasn't any better and maybe it was worse. It was four or five days before things got any better. And after I slapped you that first night when you started screaming, you calmed way down and just slept. So we've kept you here for these last two weeks. It's a good thing you finally woke up all the way because even though you ate when we brought you food, I was getting worried you might go into a coma or something with the way you would go right back to sleep every time."

By this point, she had finished feeding me my soup. She wiped my face, set the tray back on the desk, then sat back down on the bed. Her eyes were squinting slightly and, because of the way the corner of her mouth was curling up, I couldn't tell if she was studying me for something or if she was just mocking me.

"So what's the deal, are you crazy or what?" she finally asked.

I tried to say no, but couldn't. As she had been talking, I had become more and more emotional. I simply could not believe what I had heard, that there could still be such good in the world after having had everything I'd believed in blown up before my eyes. I was too choked up with gratitude for these women, especially this one, to say anything. I even felt my eyes begin to get a little teary. In the end, all I could manage was to shake my head side to side in answer to her question.

"Well, I can see that you're different than when you came here just by the look in your eyes. They looked completely wild before. And then there was all that stuff you kept screaming and yelling at first about love being dead and life being over for you. I swear, if you hadn't calmed down after I slapped you and if I hadn't felt a little sorry for you, I would have packed you into the car and hauled you to the crazy house myself, riot or no riot."

She shook her head and laughed. It was strange, and I couldn't have said just why, but I really liked her right then, especially because I knew that she meant what she said about taking me to the crazy house. She stood up, walked to the door, then turned back around. She leaned forward and smiled playfully while resting her right cheek on the door jam, making the first wholly feminine gesture she had made since she had come in.

"I never thought you were completely gone," she said after watching me for a moment or two. "I don't know why, I just didn't. Besides, I wanted to hear how the hell you got where Mama and Aunt Juanitá found you anyway."

I wanted to speak, and I even opened my mouth, but she stopped me.

"Now don't say anything," she snapped, shaking the smile from her face as she pulled herself erect. "You may not be crazy, but you've certainly been sick, and you don't need to go and tire yourself out. You rest here and be quiet. There'll be plenty of time for telling me your little story later."

She turned and shut the door behind her so sharply that I started as I had with the old woman earlier. My heart raced in my breast when she was gone. At first, my mind kept up with my heart, skipping over all the things I'd just heard. But, eventually, I started thinking about this woman I had just met. She was obviously not highly-educated and sometimes had too gruff a manner. But for some inexplicable reason, I really wanted her to like me. She was not beautiful, but I found myself very attracted to her. This feeling overwhelmed me to such a degree that even I found it strange.

But I didn't have the energy to analyze it. My stomach, though still weak, was full, and I was tired from the exertion it had taken to concentrate on all that had just been presented to me. I heeded her advice and closed my eyes for a rest. Very soon, I was sleeping more peacefully than I think I had slept since I was a baby.

In the ensuing weeks, with the nursing of Mama (as I too eventually came to call the old lady who'd first brought me the soup), Gabriella (the younger one), and even Aunt Juanitá (though the latter did this begrudgingly at first), I fully recovered from my trauma. Gabriella took care of me the most, as (I eventually discovered from Mama) she had from the beginning. After her initial prodding, I told her everything about how I'd gotten where I was when Mama and Aunt Juanitá found me. She could hardly believe the things I told her. Her responses varied.

"You are *crazy!* I should have taken you to the nuthouse."

Or: "You are so *stupid!* How could you think such a thing?"

And: "If I were her, I would have done more than kick you there!"

But she always came back, reminded me where I had left off, and told me to tell her everything, which I did without delay. I left nothing out, not even things I felt ashamed or embarrassed about in hindsight. Each word I spoke was like a weight being lifted from my soul. She laughed and gasped and shook her head and even pinched me once (at the part where I watched Ned and Charlotte from the bushes), though not very hard. I think she even cried a little, though she swore she had just gotten something in her eye. When I finally had told her everything, she just looked at me with a very calm expression for a long time without saying anything.

"Well," she finally said, "I guess you started out searching for this one woman, but it looks like you've ended up with me instead."

Here she smiled slyly and winked. An electric thrill shot through me, and I went weak as a virgin being served to King Kong. She stood up, took off her clothes, then got into bed, and took possession of me, body and soul.

~

SHE NOW RUNS MY LIFE in nearly all respects: when I go to bed, when I wake up, when I eat, how much TV and reading I get, which is almost none of the last as she is convinced it is what caused my "craziness." She took all my money away from me, investing a lot of it in blue chip stocks and municipal bonds. The rest she put into a chain of upscale, carry-out burrito restaurants, an idea she hatched very soon after I told her of my wealth. She makes me work six days a week, taking me daily to one of our shops to do "grunt work," as she calls it. She said it would help me get my strength back; but whatever strength I had lost I regained in the first few months of work, and she still makes me do it.

Only on Sunday do I rest. But never by myself. She takes me to the beach or the mountains or somewhere else in the greater Los Angeles area. Sometimes she just drives me around. She sold my Beauty (which pained me some, since we'd been through so much together) and bought a well-maintained late-seventies model convertible Cadillac, a car she had coveted since her early teens. We spent many Sundays cruising around in the weeks after the riot, looking at all the damage and scouting for locations for restaurants.

Of course, I still suffer. Gabriella and Aunt Juanitá hurt my feelings often. Not a moment passes when I am gazing pensively out some window before one or the other of them yells at me that if I don't have something to do, she can find something for me. I know I am appreciated to a certain extent. Mama, in her quiet way, is my main source of solicitude. And when no one is around, Gabriella shows herself to be her mother's daughter. But I still can't help feeling misunderstood at times. Sometimes, when I am through with a hard day of hauling supplies from the storerooms and clearing tables (I'm not allowed to take orders from customers), I feel spent and abused and spend the whole trip home in sullen silence until she explodes because I haven't responded to her questions about how my day went.

And yet, I know she loves me. She will allow no one to speak to me the way she does (save Aunt Juanitá) and, in fact, commands the same respect for me that she requires others to give her. Once, she overheard one of the cooks questioning my manhood to my face (she informed me of this as my grasp of vernacular Spanish remains tenuous) and fired him on the spot, spewing a litany of insults at him which brought a smile and a blush to all Spanish speakers in the restaurant. When asked, though she rarely is, she tells people that I am the one who chooses to work. But she and I know different.

And every night after she has gone over the numbers for the day, she comes to our room silently and undresses, then approaches me in the darkness. Unsure at first, she touches my leg or arm lightly, which I move to let her know I'm awake. Then she slides into bed, takes me into her arms and ravages my body to its undeniable pleasure. Afterwards, she rocks me slowly as she asks me in hushed tones how I could have stayed away so long. These things keep me with her and something else, something undefinable that she stirs within me.

I know it is not what I thought destiny held for me. But it is what I have, and I am not inclined to risk it for more, even if I could believe again as I did before. What I have is enough. Oh yes, I wonder about that other girl. Even now, I am thinking about what might have happened if I'd have found her, say, five or ten years sooner... Could I have saved her? Would she have been able to see me any differently? Or would she have shown me in the same stark, unbearable way the chasm that separated us and that separates even the truest of lovers... But Gabriella is calling me to dinner now, and I can tell by her tone she is not in the mood to be kept waiting.

Made in the USA
Columbia, SC
21 April 2025